Also by Ellis Blackwood

"Among the finest historical cozy mysteries of our time" – *Cozy Crime Reads*

The Samuel Pepys Mysteries
Mr Pepys's Stolen Diaries (ellisblackwood.com)
Book 1: The Brampton Witch Murders
Book 2: The Plague Doctor Murders
Book 3: The Coffee House Murders
Book 4: The King's Court Murders
Book 5: The Frost Fair Murders
Book 6: The Drury Lane Murders
Book 7: The Brampton Ghost Murders
Book 8: The Crown Jewels Murders
Book 9: Jacob's Last Standish

The Quill & Page Victorian Mysteries

Book I: The Belgravia Phantom (summer 2026)
Book II: The Whitechapel Orphan (summer 2026)

The Drury Lane Murders

The Samuel Pepys Mysteries Book 6

Ellis Blackwood

Vintage Mystery Press

Paperback ISBN: 978-1-0687027-5-4

Cover design, editorial & historical fact-checking: Tim Brown, A.S.C. (Rtd).

Masks cover image licensed from EmbossedGifts on etsy.com.

Ghost image licensed from slowbuzzstudio on stock.adobe.com.

For Withnail and Monty, inspiration for so many of my characters.

All alone to the King's playhouse, and there did happen to sit just before Mrs. Pierce, and Mrs. Knepp, who pulled me by the hair; and so I addressed myself to them, and talked to them all the intervals of the play, and did give them fruit.
From the diary of Samuel Pepys

Scan for website and social media links

Contents

Chapter One

The Foal

Jacob Standish wished he had never rummaged in his mother's armoire. And he dearly wished he had resisted the urge to try on her old chopines. How did ladies walk in such monstrous contraptions, he had wondered, as he tottered about with all the grace of a new-born foal.

He was tall enough as it was; a further ten inches off the floor, he had felt as if he were flying. Until his ankle gave way, that is, and he toppled with a shriek and a *thump*. The ridiculous shoes had suited him no better than Lady Honoria's hats.

But he was bored.

So bored, pacing the hollowness of his family's grand townhouse on Strand Lane, keenly aware of the dolorous echo of his every lumpen step.

Alone in the parlour the previous night, restless before the fire, he had taken to draping blankets over the family portraits. Those dreadful beady eyes bored into him.

Jacob craved action. How he longed to team up once more with his fellow inquisitor, Abigail Harcourt, in the employ of his mentor, Mr Samuel Pepys.

Their investigation into murder at the Thames Frost Fair had concluded more than a week ago. Mr Pepys had hinted at a new case - something afoot amid one of those London theatres Jacob had heard so much about - but had then been called away to Brampton, where his father lay unwell.

Abby, meanwhile, had been reunited with her brother, Will, after years of estrangement, and seemed to be making up for lost time. When Jacob had called at her tiny lodgings, in the same naval estate as Mr Pepys, he had found a note pinned to her door.

Visiting the Frost Fair

He knew why. Will had a printing press set up there, in a booth on Temple Street, fleecing Londoners only too willing to part with a shilling in exchange for a scrap of card.

He did not begrudge her the reunion. Abby and Will had been tight as thieves growing up, until… Such a sorrowful, sordid tale, he did not care to recollect.

All in the past now, apparently, after Will had risked his life to save hers, and she had accepted his excuses for what - in Jacob's eyes - was craven disloyalty.

He could have joined her at the fair… yet had lacked the desire. He had seen past the gaiety to the greed of men and the perils of the frost. If he never witnessed another Frost Fair in his lifetime, it might be too soon.

It mattered no longer. His maidservant, who visited daily and generally cowered when he tried to speak with her, had informed him lately that the ice was breaking up and the booths were vanishing as quickly as they had appeared.

Nay, he did not begrudge Abby her happiness, yet still he missed her. His chest felt somehow hollow. She had been a constant colleague and companion these past four months, ever since they had been thrown together, and now she had been ripped away by another: *cursed Will Harcourt.*

Jacob rose, tentatively testing his throbbing ankle, gripped by a sense of purpose. The renewed vigour felt good.

Carefully, he replaced the ghastly chopines precisely as he had found them, knowing his mother's fastidious nature. Not that she ever visited.

Then he strode to his chamber. Hang the dreadful chill outside – he would try Abby once more. If the carnival had indeed dispersed, she may well have returned home.

Perhaps Mr Pepys, also?

Chapter Two

A Visitor

Jacob pulled on his thick woollen coat, straightened his tangled periwig and topped it with a wide-brimmed hat. At the door, he steeled himself before lifting the latch.

The weather hit him like an escaping cart-horse. He had not been outside in some while and, even if the Thames ice had abandoned its hold, the wind still cut clean through him. Hastily, he clamped his hat to his head, turned right and peered up and down The Strand. A mangy dog was pawing at the filthy slush for anything edible, oblivious to the hackney coaches splashing past.

To his right, the tower of St Clement Danes church stood silent and grey. He stared at it for a while, lost in jumbled thoughts, until its bell chimed, and he shook himself alert.

Feeling his pasty cheeks growing rosy, Jacob plumped up his cravat and made for Temple Bar.

He and Abby had trudged the same route, he remembered, to witness the opening day of the Frost Fair. Then, the mood had been one of promise; today, he hoped, might realise the same.

The sight of London levelled by fire never ceased to distress him, as he feared it ever would, until the city was rebuilt. The blanketed snow, which had lately lent the ruins some grace, had now all but melted away, allowing the full horror to return.

Incredibly, despite the worst attempts of the elements, there were people out there labouring, desperate to begin again. The sound of hammer blows and scything saws whipped past Jacob's numbed ears as he swallowed hard and headed for the river.

It took him off his planned path - along Fleet Street, over Fleet Bridge, then onto Thames Street toward Mr Pepys's on Seething Lane - but he wanted to see the river for himself. It held memories.

When he reached the southern end of Middle Temple Lane, there it was: the full width of the vast waterway before him, and stretching far off to the east.

His maidservant had been right. The Frost Fair was gone, as if it had been merely a dream. A dark, unholy dream, as it became. It occurred to him again that he might well have died out there.

The Thames had returned to its usual muddy brown, though it teemed with jagged shards and drifting sheets of ice, all moving sluggishly toward London Bridge. No Thames waterman would dare launch a wherry into that. The little craft would be battered and upended within yards of the bank, and its master would face a cold and lonely death.

Such a river, it occurred to Jacob, was more powerful than any act of God. It had seen off plague and fire, and would endure into a future he could not begin to imagine.

"Fare, good sir?"

Jacob turned. A hackney coachman had halted his horses behind him, unnoticed. One of the beasts side-eyed him with disdain, and he cast it a belligerent sneer.

These fellows were meant to wait for fares at designated stands, but since the fire had taken to plying their trade as they pleased.

"You look cold," the coachman persisted, waving a hand toward his door.

Jacob required no second bidding.

"Mr Pepys!" he exclaimed, upon seeing his employer rise to greet him at Seething Lane.

Only when he noticed Pepys flinch as he approached at pace, beaming rabidly, did he grind to a halt and lower his arms. "'Tis good to see you, sir," he added, with a little more decorum, and bowed.

"Indeed, Mr Standish," Pepys intoned with mock solemnity, before rounding his dining table, dark eyes shining, to grasp the younger man by the forearms. "And how mighty pleased I am to see you, sir!"

Jacob, who was a head taller than Pepys, twitched. Mr Samuel Pepys, Clerk of the Acts to the Navy Board, was pleased - *to see him.* The only other person he could recall voicing the same was Abby.

How fortunate he was, he realised, to have stumbled into this inquisitor lark. It gave him more than merely a trade. It had returned to him his dignity.

Releasing his grip, Pepys motioned toward a place at the end of the table. "I discovered another acquaintance of yours."

In his blind haste, Jacob had not noticed Abby, and when he did so - he could not halt them - he felt tears well in his eyes. Blinking furiously, his lids swallowed them down.

"A-Abigail," he stammered, as she flung herself at him, clinging so tightly that Pepys was minded to harrumph.

Jacob felt so happy he was fit to burst.

While the reunited inquisitors and their employer caught up on recent events, Mary Blythe, the kitchen maid, furnished them with cold mutton, trenchers of bread and warmed, spiced ale. Jacob, who was accustomed to ignoring waiting staff, cast her a faint smile, and she stifled a giggle, pointedly eyeing Abby, who winked back.

Noticing the exchange, Pepys asked, "Am I interrupting something?" before continuing the stories of his father John's gout, and his sister Paulina's latest unsuitable suitor. As Pepys's gaze disappeared behind his tankard while he paused to guzzle, Abby and Jacob shot each other a knowing look.

It felt like old times.

"What of you, Jacob?" Pepys asked, when finally he was done.

Suddenly aware of the sprain in his ankle, Jacob coughed lightly. "Nought of any import, sir, I fear."

Pepys shrugged. "And you, Abigail? How goes it with your brother, William?"

Grinning brightly, Abby launched into tales of aiding Will at his press on Temple Street and their reignited friendship. Jacob, once listening keenly, found his attention waning.

"Is that not marvellous, Jacob?" Pepys asked.

It was only the sound of his name that lured him from his thoughts. "Hnn?"

"Is it not marvellous that Abigail here has rediscovered happiness with a brother she had long since abandoned?"

Jacob managed a nod as Pepys added, "Thanks in no small part to my persistence as intermediary?"

Abby let out a single high-pitched laugh, which she was obliged to disguise as hiccups.

"When last we met, sir, here in this very room," Jacob said, "you mentioned our next investigation. You asked if had visited the King's Playhouse?"

"Ah! So I did, Jacob."

As a man who embraced life's pleasures, Mr Pepys adored the theatre. He would, he told them, attend several plays each month - each week, if he could find the time (the cost no longer being a concern).

It set him apart from his inquisitors. Abby could never have afforded a seat, even in the upper gallery among the apprentices and artisans, while Jacob had never seen the appeal of men prancing about on a stage, occasionally bursting into song.

In Pepys's company, however, he preferred to affect an interest. "I heard, sir, that Mr Shakeshaft's works are greatly admired," he said, cocking an unruly eyebrow.

Pepys puffed out his cheeks. "Shakeshaft?"

"I think he means Mr Shakespeare, sir," Abby said.

Jacob's smugness evaporated as he blustered an excuse.

Pepys smiled. "I have witnessed several of William Shakespeare's plays, Jacob, with mixed blessings. Othello and Macbeth did both move me greatly, however the less said about Romeo and Juliet, the better." Abby opened her mouth to speak, but he carried on. "One of the worst plays I have seen in my life."

Abby paused to confirm her employer had finished. "And our investigation, sir?"

"Ah!" Pepys slapped his thigh. "Your *investigation*."

Noting his inquisitors' ignorance of theatrical matters, he began at the beginning.

There were, he explained, two principal patent theatre companies in London. The King's Company operated out of the King's Playhouse off Drury Lane. The Duke's Company, under the patronage of Charles's brother, James, staged their plays at the Duke's Playhouse on Lincoln's Inn Field.

The King's Company focused more on traditional productions, while the Duke's tended toward innovation. "However, both are of equal merit," Pepys added.

"You do not prefer one over the other?" Jacob asked.

"The last play I attended was Mr Boyle's Mustapha. It did please me mightily. Such noble construction." Then suddenly he stood and began quoting, "*I am for Mustapha's true love in debt, which I will never pay with counterfeit…*"

Abby cut in, "At which playhouse was this, sir?"

Briefly befuddled, Pepys sat heavily and took a slug of ale, wrinkling his nose when he discovered it had gone cold. "At the Duke's. However," he sighed, "'tis the King's Playhouse that does concern me."

The King's Company, he said, was owned by a gentleman named Thomas Tresillion, who was also a noted courtier and Groom of the King's Bedchamber. Pepys had heard rumours, during his many visits to the King's Playhouse, of unrest among the players, amid accusations of financial impropriety.

"Who told you these rumours?" Jacob asked.

"The playhouse operates a system of shareholders," Pepys replied. "Each invests money and receives a share of takings from the performances. At least, that is the theory. Shareholders, I hear tell, are not receiving their due monies. Threats have been made, and aspersions cast. The actors, 'tis said, are plotting rebellion."

"Which actors, sir?" Abby asked. "Who are these shareholders?"

Pepys tapped the table several times. "*That* is the question, Abigail. Certain of Tresillion's actors own shares, I am told, yet he refuses to divulge their names. Meanwhile, the actors themselves remain tight-lipped. If one learned another's share was greater, all Hell would break loose. Such are the pride and envy of the theatre."

Pepys sat back, arms folded.

Financial impropriety was not what Jacob had had in mind when Pepys had first mentioned rum doings on the stage. The failed purser's apprentice had no head for figures, nor any great desire to correct it. Money meant little to him - perhaps because had never been short of it, thanks to family connections. His late father, Sir Miles Standish, had been a high-ranking colleague of Pepys's at the Navy Board, and his modest estate in Greenwich attested to the family's wealth.

"These threats, Mr Pepys," Jacob said. "Are they mortal threats?"

Abby glanced at him, knowing precisely the workings of his mind. Previously, Pepys had sent them both on a mission to recover his lost pocket watch, which had appealed to neither.

Fortunately, the case had subsequently darkened.

"I know not the detail, Jacob," Pepys replied. "That is for you to discover, as my personal inquisitor." He turned to Abby. "As my personal *inquisitors*. You know…?" Pepys inhaled, smiling to himself. "My neighbour, Sir William Penn, asked after your services recently. I was saddened to inform him you were far too busy toiling on my behalf."

His lingering grin suggested that, on the contrary, he was delighted. Then his expression hardened, and he eyed his inquisitors in turn. "You will remember, I am sure, that you work exclusively for me?"

Both inquisitors nodded earnestly.

"Why does this particular matter concern you so, sir?" Abby asked.

Pepys pulled himself upright. "Why, Abigail, 'tis the King's own playhouse. I should have thought it obvious?"

Abby suppressed a knowing smile. Indeed it was: her employer desired a return to the King's good books, after the dreadful saga at court when Pepys had been arrested for a crime he did not commit.

Downstairs, there came a knock at the door.

"How do you propose we set about this new investigation?" she asked.

"We shall attend a play," said Pepys. "At the King's Playhouse."

Abby, who had hoped as much, clapped her hands joyfully. "When?"

"On this very afternoon. His Majesty's Company is performing The Maid's Tragedy, by Francis Beaumont and John Fletcher, and I shall…"

A figure appeared at the top of the stairs. "William!" Pepys cried.

"Will!" said Abby, rising to greet her brother.

Jacob barely managed a polite tip of the head.

Chapter Three

Plans Rewritten

Will Harcourt shared the same piercing turquoise eyes as his sister, and their hair was a similar orange-red, though hers was the fierier. In manner, Jacob considered, they could not have been more different.

To him, Abby was keen-minded, resourceful, gentle and honest - if a little over-assertive at times, particularly with lofty gentlemen. Will was too brash by half: a lout, disloyal and untrustworthy, and undeserving of her affections. That his first impression of Abby's brother had been that he was "bright and industrious"… well, he had tempered that since rethinking the young man's behaviour.

Or so he told himself.

Bade to take a seat at the table, Will grinned impishly at his sister as he shovelled a handful of leftover meat into his mouth, to Pepys's evident consternation.

When he proceeded to wash that down with a swig from Jacob's tankard, she widened her eyes at him. "Behave yourself, brother," she told him quietly.

"I was invited," Will said, waving a finger towards their host.

"Em, how goes the printing business, William?" enquired Pepys, for whom polite discourse was second nature.

"It boomed, sir." Swallowing loudly, Will smacked his lips. "Till the ice broke."

Pepys coughed. "Indeed. And what will you do now?"

Will reached for a second helping of mutton, ignoring Jacob's pained expression. 'Tis why I am here, sir. When I couldn't find Abby at her lodgings, I hoped I would find her here. And, lo, there she is!"

When Abby tilted her head, he continued, "I was hoping she'd help me set up the press back at my shop. Now it's been returned from the Frost Fair."

All three men turned their gaze on Abby.

"But I've been charged with…" she said.

Jacob cut her off. "As Mr Pepys's personal inquisitors, we have been charged with investigating financial impropriety…"

Will snorted. "'E can barely say it, let alone investigate it!"

Ignoring Jacob's splutters, he turned back to his sister. "Say you'll help, sis. Only you know that press as well as I do. 'Twas our…"

"Aye, 'twas our father's," she added, dropping her head.

Jacob looked at her askance. *How could she not defend me?* "We have a duty to Mr Pepys," he pointed out, voice rising with indignation.

Pepys nodded. "I am minded to concur with Jacob, since…"

Slipping off his chair, Will bowed to his host. "Mr Pepys, your reputation for wisdom and generosity precedes you, sir. My sister has not the superlatives to describe your good character."

When Will dropped to one knee, Jacob sighed petulantly.

"Sir, I beg you…" Will said.

Pepys, blushing, raised a palm. "Abigail, I cannot withhold you from aiding your brother in his time of need. This matter of mine can wait. I am sure…"

"But, sir…" Now Jacob, too, was out of his chair.

Pepys silenced him also. "Pray, let me finish, Jacob. I am sure that Mr Standish and I can attend the performance today and ask sufficient questions to begin the investigation. We may then reunite with Abigail to pass on our discoveries, once William's work at his shop is completed."

Tutting under his breath, Jacob retook his seat. On the one hand, he would be accompanying Pepys alone, with all the honour and responsibility that entailed. On the other, Will appeared to have won.

"Does that suit you, Abigail?" Pepys asked, peering kindly.

She looked from Pepys to her brother and smiled. "I'm much obliged to you, sir," she said, then added eagerly, "I'll make it up to you. I'll…"

But Pepys waved her exhortations aside. "I am well aware of your attention to duty, fear not. Else I would not have offered you this opportunity."

"When we're finished," Will piped up, "perhaps I could join you? On this investigation? Being an inquisitor might be in the blood, eh, Abby?"

When she failed to reply, he cocked a thumb at Jacob. "I couldn't do no worse'n this lump, could I?" He chuckled, leering. "I've heard about you. Always fallin' over."

Jacob swivelled to face Abby, brown eyes blazing.

"I told him in jest!" she blurted. "Did I not, Will?" But her brother only smirked. "*Will?*"

"Oh aye," he obliged, oozing sarcasm. "Only in jest."

Pepys, eyeing Jacob anxiously, placed both palms flat on the table. "I shall not be requiring a third inquisitor. You would do well, William, to focus upon your printing duties."

Chapter Four

Theatrical Discourse

Via a servant, Mr Pepys had arranged for a hackney coach to arrive at Seething Lane at one of the clock. It would allow ample time for he and Jacob to question Thomas Tresillion before the performance began at three.

Jacob was quiet - unusually so - as they clattered and lurched along Thames Street. The wind had died down, but the chill remained, inhabiting the stark wooden cab like a vengeful ghost.

Pepys broke the silence. "I would not dream of employing that young man. Since I already possess London's two finest inquisitors."

Jacob barely nodded. "Aye, sir. And I am grateful to you."

Outside, the wheels hissed through the slush.

"And I am quite sure Abigail mentioned your…" Pepys paused, wondering how best to frame his words, "*occasional mishaps* to her brother merely in jest."

Jacob forced a smile. There was no denying it: he was clumsy. "I lament the melting of the ice, sir. I felt steadier upon it than I ever do upon the city's streets."

"Do you remember…?" Pepys grinned mischievously. "Do you remember when you fell off the quayside at the King's court?" His eyes twinkled…

Then dimmed, as Jacob's downcast demeanour returned. Clearing his throat, Pepys added, "Abigail seems fond of you."

Jacob glanced up, almost too hopeful.

"Aye, Jacob. I have seen the manner in which she regards you."

"You have, sir?"

"Indeed. And now she has her brother, who vies for her attention." Pepys sucked in his lips. "Jealousy is a dread enemy, Mr Standish. You must banish him from your thoughts."

Had Jacob been privy to the contents of his employer's diary, he would have seen the hypocrisy in Pepys's - albeit kindly - words. Elizabeth Pepys need only speak to another man, and her husband would torment himself with visions of her imagined entanglement.

"Are we travelling to my residence?" Jacob asked, peering out of the window.

Having reached the western extent of Thames Street, they had turned north to cross Fleet Bridge and were now trundling east on Fleet Street. It was the precise route he had planned to take to Mr Pepys's, only in reverse.

"You live on Strand Lane, do you not?" Pepys asked.

Jacob, a tad put out that his employer had to ask, nodded curtly.

"Then you must surely have visited the King's Playhouse, which lies no more than a five-minute stroll hence?"

Does it? thought Jacob, disguising his embarrassment with a wipe of the nose.

Pepys studied the younger man. "You have visited the playhouse?"

Jacob's sheepish expression suggested otherwise. Growing up in Greenwich, as he had, then working among the seafarers at the docks, there had been no access to theatre - nor much notion of its existence.

Honest toil and loyalty to the King had been drummed into him, not the Arts.

Jacob's three sisters - Anne, Margaret and Elizabeth - had taken turns attempting to master the harpsichord, until the day their father took an axe to the thing, their tuneless dirges having addled his mind once too often.

The Standishes were not that sort of family. When the children played, the sisters would band together, while Jacob's brothers, the twins, jeered him as an outcast. Their games involved more rough-and-tumble than the staging of plays.

Pepys leapt from his seat opposite and squeezed in next to Jacob. "Oh, Jacob, the marvels you have denied yourself!"

"Indeed, sir."

"What a piece of work is man!"

Jacob shifted aside. "As I have often thought."

Pepys only edged closer. "Hamlet, Jacob!" He chortled, digging the inquisitor in the ribs. "One of Mr Shakespeare's finer plays. And Benedict Lansmere as the Prince - beyond imagination!"

"I shall bear that in mind, sir. And today's play? This Maid's Tragedy?"

"I have seen it before." Pepys patted Jacob's knee. "It… had its moments. Today, we shall witness it together."

Chapter Five

Tresillion

Once through the arch at Temple Bar, instead of continuing along The Strand to Jacob's, the coach veered right onto Drury Lane.

With a "Woah!" to his horses, the coachman soon drew to a halt. "Theatre Royal!" he announced.

"He has brought us to the wrong theatre," Jacob hissed.

Pepys chuckled. "The King's Playhouse goes by many names, the Theatre Royal among them. Come!" As the door opened, he rose with a stoop to avoid striking his head on the cab roof.

The palatial red-brick townhouses lining the street were familiar to Jacob, with their classical columns and lead guttering. He had strolled up Drury Lane before, whiling away the hours after he had been dismissed from the navy, following a potentially calamitous miscalculation of rations.

As then, the street was busy. Hawkers with baskets of fruit, sweetmeats and roasted chestnuts cried out;

shopfronts displayed all manner of wares - periwigs, prints, pies - while liveried men carrying sedan chairs trotted past, perfumed ladies peeking out from behind curtains.

What Jacob could not see, however, was any sign of a theatre.

Turning, he noticed Pepys head into an alleyway between buildings, and quickly followed.

"The King's Playhouse cannot be seen from Drury Lane," Pepys said, reading Jacob's mind. His voice echoed off the high brick walls on either side. "'Twas built on the site of a stable yard barely four years ago, among so many clustered buildings. All belong to the Dukes of Bedford, who leased the site to Thomas Tresillion."

At the end, barely lit by oil lamps in the dank, chill passageway, was a plain door set into a looming timber structure.

"The rear entrance," Pepys said, rapping confidently on the door. "Perfect for our purposes."

Chiming bells told them it was well past the second hour.

As footsteps approached from within, Pepys turned to Jacob and whispered, "I am beginning to feel like an inquisitor, Jacob, and do believe I am envious."

The door was opened by a man wearing a tattered leather jerkin over a stained linen shirt. A long, pale scar cut across the side of his scalp, just above the ear, where no hair grew. He glared at them with suspicion, as if peering into blackness.

"Wha'd'yer want?" he asked. "Entrance is on Bridges Street. This is the actors' entrance."

Jacob noticed a dagger in his belt. His hands were calloused and his knuckles swollen.

"Mr Samuel Pepys," Pepys replied, undaunted by the ruffian's demeanour. "And Mr Jacob Standish. We are here to see Mr Tresillion."

"For what purpose?"

Pepys stiffened. "I fail to see what business that is of yours, Mr...?"

"Tibbet." It came out like a gruff frog.

"Mr Tibbet."

Tibbet nodded and stepped aside. "Aye. You're right. 'Taint my business. I've enough to cope with already."

"And you are?" Jacob asked.

Tibbet, thick-set and menacing, looked the inquisitor up and down. "I told yer. Tibbet."

"Indeed!" Jacob laughed nervously. "I was referring to your purpose here. At the theatre."

"Why? What's it to you?"

Pepys hastily cut in, "Where shall we find Mr Tresillion?"

They were in a narrow corridor running the width of the building, musty-smelling and dingy. Opposite was a door, and another at the far end, which Tibbet gestured towards. "Tresillion's office. You'll find him in there, all aflutter no doubt."

With that, he slipped through the door opposite. As it opened, Jacob caught a glimpse of figures in stage attire beyond, and the murmur of voices rehearsing speeches.

Tresillion's office looked as if it had been ransacked. Ledgers, papers and thick volumes lay scattered across the desk, strewn about the floor, and heaped haphazardly on shelves that lined the timber walls. There was one window, shuttered, behind the manager of the King's Company, which Jacob supposed looked out over the stage from the rear.

A blackened charcoal brazier beside the desk gave out a grudging heat. Beneath it was a heavy wooden chest, ribbed with ironwork and sealed with a padlock.

Pepys had knocked and Tresillion had bade them enter with a distracted call, yet the manager did not look up when they entered.

Having picked their way through piled papers, Jacob and Pepys presented themselves before the desk and Pepys cleared his throat.

"If 'tis pay you're after, Peregrine, then I suggest you leave a grievance in writing and return to your duties. Our performance begins within the half-hour." Tresillion, still intent on his scribbling, made an impatient shooing gesture.

"Mr Tresillion, 'tis I, Samuel Pepys. I bring with me London's finest inquisitor, Mr Jacob Standish."

Jacob, fighting a wilful grin, felt a shiver ripple down his spine.

With a sigh, Tresillion looked up, peering through the office gloom.

"Pepys? Gah! Why did you not say so?" He removed a goblet from his desk and set in on the floor, out of sight.

Pepys shuffled his feet.

"London's finest inquisitor, you say?" Tresillion added, appraising Jacob. "And what, pray, is his purpose?"

Thomas Tresillion was a small but wiry old fellow, swallowed in a thick black coat with dull braid. His grey periwig was perched on his head like an afterthought, and his face was etched with furrows. Dark bags beneath his eyes told of sleepless nights.

His pallid skin seemed almost translucent, and Jacob fancied he could make out the contours of the bones beneath.

"Mr Standish is my personal inquisitor, Thomas," Pepys explained. "He investigates dark dealings on my behalf. He has…"

"Then why bring him here, to my theatre?" Tresillion snapped, suddenly animated. "We have no dark dealings here. Only those writ by the finest authors of their age."

Pepys chuckled unconvincingly. "Indeed, Thomas. And you know full well how highly I regard the work of you and your estimable company. Why, not a month past, I saw The Scornful Lady here, the part being played most admirably by Franny Jenkins. I commend you upon it, sir. 'Twas writ, I believe by the same gentlemen who did write The Maid's Tragedy, which we are about to see…"

He was still extolling the virtues of The Scornful Lady when he felt Jacob's boot tap against his.

"Sir," Jacob cut in, "should we not speak of the rumours of financial misdealing? 'Tis, after all, the reason we are here."

Tresillion rose from his seat, hands on desk, eyes blazing. "Rumours? Of financial misdealing?"

Pepys turned to Jacob, who swallowed drily.

"We wish only to help, Thomas," said Pepys. "I think of the King alone, whose illustrious company this is."

Tresillion's lips curled into a contemptuous smile. "What is your relation to His Majesty, Pepys?"

Pepys looked momentarily nonplussed. "I am Clerk of the Acts to his Navy Board, as well you know. We have made acquaintance at his court on many occasions."

"Aye. I, who am Groom of the King's Bedchamber, privy to his innermost thoughts, and to whom he granted a patent, entrusting me with one of this city's two theatrical companies. Who did receive the other patent, do you remember? Was it you, Pepys?"

Pepys could only raise an eyebrow.

"Nay, 'twas not." Stepping back, Tresillion swept a hand across his chair. "Nevertheless, come, take my seat. With your head for figures and knowledge of theatre, no doubt Londoners shall flock here in their droves and our counting house shall overflow. You've watched hundreds of plays, I daresay." He paused, smiling beatifically. "I merely staged them."

Jacob physically winced as Tresillion delivered his *coup de grâce*. Tired and flimsy as the old manager appeared, he had not lost his backbone.

All the while, the noise coming through the wooden walls of the office had grown, rising as the audience filled the theatre to witness The Maid's Tragedy. Jacob had expected something more reverent, but the sound was raucous - bawdy laughter and catcalls.

He wondered what it looked like out there.

Pepys, who had turned puce, sighed exasperatedly. "Mr Tresillion…"

"Mr Pepys," Tresillion cut in, retaking his seat. "Perhaps you could tell me the content of these rumours you heard, which besmirch my good character so? That I may address them."

"Monies have gone missing, sir, and actors have not been paid their due share of the takings."

"Nought but slander and make-believe!" Tresillion breathed heavily. "Which scobberlotcher told you such untruths? Was it Orange Bess, who has a gob the size of Cripplegate? Or Tibbet, perhaps, who could find fault with Heaven itself?" He narrowed his eyes at Pepys. "Marwood? Lansmere?"

"I cannot reveal my sources," said Pepys. "Loyalty, I am sure we can agree, is a precious commodity."

"Indeed. And in short supply among my treacherous company of thieves." Tresillion retrieved the goblet he had hidden, and took a healthy swig. "Actors have bemoaned their wages since plays were first staged, Mr Pepys. They are prone to exaggeration and wear many faces. Which one would you believe?"

Pepys glanced about the room, unable to disguise his disgust. He was a man of order, not disarray.

Jacob could tell that he was riled.

"How do you expect to maintain accurate accounts when… when…" Pepys trailed off.

Jacob lifted his hand. "Sir, if I may…?"

Tresillion spluttered. "You're said to be London's finest inquisitor, Standish," Tresillion shot Pepys a sceptical glance. "Or are you also merely playing the part?"

Jacob adjusted his periwig. "Mr Pepys tells me the actors have shares in the King's Company."

"Not each and every actor," Tresillion said. "Only the finest."

"And that, sir, was my question. Which of them hold shares?"

Slapping his desk, the old manager shook his head in dismay. "Do I barge into your house, demanding to know your household finances? To see your ledgers, and the amounts you pay your servants?" He waited for Jacob to confirm he did not. "Are you the King?"

Jacob turned to Pepys, who shrugged.

Tresillion's jaw tightened, and he bared his teeth as he spoke. "This is the King's Company - the King's, mark me - and I'll be damned before I answer to you, sir!"

A thumping came on the wall behind him. "'Tis almost time, Mr Tresillion," came the muffled voice, which Jacob recognised as Tibbet's.

Tresillion rose abruptly, sending his chair toppling backwards. "Begone! Both of you!"

Chapter Six

Return to Bleak Alley

The last time Abby had set eyes on her childhood home, a long while ago now, it had been with a backward glance. Her own brother, Will, had betrayed their father, Ambrose, and she had fled, certain she would never again bear witness to its crooked walls and tattered thatch.

It had felt good. Cleansing.

Yet here she was, with Will at her side, gazing once more at the old door.

She remembered the latch - how stiff it was, how the door had to be wrenched forward by the handle before it would release. And there, in the weathered, cracked wood, the initial and date she had scratched when she was but a child.

A 1656

She would have been nine years old.

It brought a lump to her throat. So many memories of this house, and of Southwark.

The smells were the same - the salt tang of the nearby river mingling with the stench of every facet of human labour - worse than she remembered, yet surely unchanged.

Tooley Street with its inns and houses of ill repute, lay behind them; they had taken it to reach The Maze and Beak Alley. "Bleak Alley", as she and Will had known it without judgement or sorrow.

The place simply was bleak, and they had learned to cope and later embrace it. They knew every neighbour - every porter, brickmaker, seamstress and tanner - and any one of them would rush to help in another's hour of need. Even those prone to skullduggery.

Looking up, Abby saw her brother's sign fixed to the wall.

W. Wrathbone. Printer
At the sign of The Phoenix

The last time she had seen it was at the Thames Frost Fair. A sense of unease crept over her like a shadow, and she shuddered.

"You keep that evil man's name," she said, referring to Wrathbone, the man whose name Will had taken.

Will followed her gaze. "I can't afford a new one," he told her. "Don't let it concern you."

But I do, she thought.

Stepping inside, she let out a deep, juddering sigh.

There stood her father's solid oak printing press, just as it always had been - almost part of the fabric of the building. The smell of the ink assaulted her nostrils, bringing with it a wave of forgotten childhood. She and Will had explored every inch of that contraption as small children, undaunted by its sharp corners and moving parts.

There, the fireplace, where her mother, Mary, had suspended spits and pots to cook their meals, the tantalising aromas causing the children to sit and stare into the flames.

There, the wooden stairs leading to the upper floor among the roof beams, where the family had slept on straw infested with rodents, wrapped in blankets and snuggled together against England's harsh winters, while the rain came in. The same space where she had discovered the pamphlets condemning their father. Pamphlets Will had printed and secreted there.

Her brother tapped her on the shoulder. "Tell me your thoughts," he said gently, peering into those eyes the same hue as his own.

She could only shake her head.

He reached for her hand, and reluctantly she accepted it. "Why so low?" he asked. "We've discoursed since our reunion, and you seemed happy."

"You've brought me here," she said quietly.

"It's not changed much. Keep expecting Mother and Father to walk in." Will chuckled.

She glanced across at the press. "Looks ready to print."

"Aye, 'tis. Should be setting her to work again to-morrow. Mr Eversleigh has more of his scathing broadsides to print. They're…" He paused, studying her face. "What troubles you?"

She gazed upwards. "You do, Will. You trouble me. You brought me here, claiming you needed help with the press. Yet here I am, and now you tell me it needs no setting up. That 'tis ready to churn out these broadsides of your precious Mr Eversleigh."

He squeezed her hand, and spoke plaintively. "I wanted to see you again, Abby. Forgive me if you feel I've brought you here under false pretences. If I did, 'twas only that you might revisit our home. Share memories."

She shoved him in the chest and, unprepared, he stumbled backwards, just managing to plant a foot before he fell. "My memories of this place are such that I'd rather forget. D'you remember printing those pamphlets, Will? The pamphlets that led Father to die a slow and gruesome death in the stinking Clink?"

Rubbing his cheeks vigorously, he kept his distance. "Folk change, Abby. I made mistakes, which I sorely regret."

"*Yet you keep that man's name!*" she screamed, torn between staying and breaking for the door.

Will threw up his hands. "I told you, I can't afford to change it. But I promise, the moment I'm paid, I'll have it done. Think of it…" Will motioned towards the sign that would be. "'W. Harcourt. Printer. At the sign of the Phoenix.' Harcourt - just as it used to be."

Abby dropped to her knees, bent double, and threw her arms over her head. "'At the sign of the Phoenix'," she repeated, spitting out the words. "The Righteous Flame. Those awful men…"

"I severed ties with them!" He edged closer. "Those grim days are done, believe me. I… I need your help, Abby. I need my sister."

She raised her gaze to his. That tangled mop of red hair; those watery eyes, so filled with remorse. Her Will.

And he was not done. "Remember how we were as children? We couldn't be parted. I strayed down the wrong path, I know that, and I'm dreadful sorry. But now I return. Will and Abby, once again. Think of it."

Slowly, uncertainly, she rose and moved closer to him. When they embraced, he let out a contented sigh.

She could not see, as his head came to rest on her shoulder, the smile curling on his lips.

The aromas of the boiling mutton pottage, a staple in the Harcourt household, made Abby's eyes mist over. Will had prepared the dish as their mother once had, with mutton neck, oatmeal, onions and parsnips, boiled over the fire with water drawn from the local pump.

They sat opposite one another at the table, the two spaces beside them silent and empty, as the steam rose off their plates, and they ate greedily.

"Are these plates new?" Abby asked. "They seem un-marked."

Will bit off a hunk of bread. "Aye, sis," he replied, mouth full, and held up his knife. "The knives also."

She stopped eating. "Where…"

"The money?" He swallowed. "Remember the Frost Fair? I took more coin in those few days than I would've in many months. I'm rich! Or… richer than before. Do you need any…"

"Nay, Will. I don't want your money."

After a while, he spoke. "Forgive me for keeping you from your work. At the theatre?"

She nodded.

"It sounds so invigorating, the life of an inquisitor. I envy you. Tell me another tale of your adventures."

Abby tilted her head.

He wrung his hands before her in mock-supplication. "I beg you, mistress! Tell me a tale of derring-do!"

Laughing, she relented, and began the story of the despicable Plague Doctor at Deptford docks.

When she finished, Will shook his head in admiration. Their stomachs were full, and their hearts gladdened.

"D'you not think I'd make a fine inquisitor?" he asked, and spoke over her when she tried to reply. "Remember when Neddy Rudge stole father's foolscap for his cones of roasted chestnuts? And I dusted soot on the paper drawer, and we caught him… black-handed!" Will beamed at his own wit.

Abby rose and took their plates. "This is different. These are murders, not stolen paper."

"But I solved it! I caught the thief! Think of it… Will and Abby Harcourt, London's finest inquisitors. Brother and sister. We'd be famous." He paused, eyes alive. "I could sell the press…"

"Nay, Will." She began cleaning the plates in a bucket, avoiding his gaze.

"That Jacob of yours is an oaf, is he not? You told me so yourself."

She turned sharply. "I told you he could be clumsy, that's all. He's a most excellent inquisitor."

"Do you love him?"

The question caught her off-guard, and she dropped a plate into the water. The sound seemed to echo around the room.

He clapped delightedly. "You do! I knew it!"

Hands on hips, she stood and faced him. "'Twas a foolish question. We've grown close through our work, yet not that close. Jacob is a dear friend and colleague."

Will narrowed his eyes, grinned, rose, and took her hands in his. "Harcourt and Harcourt. Inquisitors to Mr Samuel Pepys."

She pulled away. "Nay, Will. Leave it be, I tell you."

Abby was glad when Will suggested she return home, rather than sleep in her old bed. He had work coming in, he said, and expected to be at his press into the night. It would keep her awake.

She would not have slept anyway, she knew.

Their meetings since their reunion had left Abby un-settled. So much lay between them - guilt, longing, duty, anger - all tangled together, impossible to separate. And here, in this old house, there were ghosts.

Their father had been a generous and forgiving man. However grave Will's sins, she knew he would have pardoned them, and the thought steadied her. He was her younger brother, if only by a year, and that would never change.

Chapter Seven

The Tiring-House

"Not a terribly welcoming place, is it, sir? I had expected…"

"Hush, Jacob!" Pepys snapped.

Despite his shorter legs, he was leading them up Drury Lane, head down, muttering to himself and breathing heavily.

Jacob persisted, "I found Mr Tresillion rather…"

"I said, be silent!"

Taking two left turns, onto Russell Street then Bridges Street, brought them into an alleyway milling with people, hemmed in by high brick walls on either side.

Pepys barged through. Some complained, others threatened, but he was in no mood to be halted.

At the alley's end, the theatre began to rise before them – tall, topped with a lantern cupola, otherwise unremarkable. Timber-framed with rough-plastered walls, it bore a pair of stout doors, the crowd pressing eagerly inside.

"Make way, would you?" Pepys barked, pushing folk aside to reach the front of the line.

"Who's he think he is?" an old crone wondered aloud.

"Is it the King?" a neighbour asked.

"Don't look much like the King to me," the crone pointed out. "Too short."

As Pepys reached the doorway, jostled and seething, a grimy lad with a sneer - an apprentice of some sort - barred his way.

"Stand aside!" he growled.

But the lad would not move.

Sensing his moment, Jacob stepped forward, grabbed the youth by the collar, and shoved him against the wall. "This is Mr Samuel Pepys!" he announced grandly.

"Who?" someone asked.

While his employer disappeared inside, Jacob whispered to the lad, "I do beg your pardon."

He found himself in the entrance hall, packed with folk heading this way and that. Their collective warmth was immediate and welcoming. He had almost forgotten how cold he was.

Directly ahead, a solid wall blocked the view; behind it, he reasoned, must be the galleries and the stage. Corridors to either side headed around the perimeter of the theatre.

The air smelled of musty bodies, already beginning to steam.

Lost in thought, Jacob almost missed seeing Pepys head through a small arch to the right, and hurried after him.

The passage was narrow, the ceiling low. Overhead, he could hear the clumping of footsteps on wood - folk finding their seats in the gallery above. Turning to follow the south wall, he emerged at the edge of the auditorium and stopped.

The scene took his breath away.

The space opened before him like a bowl, steep-sided and swarming with people. Benches in the pit, cushioned with green baize, faced the stage. They rose in ranks on a sloping floor, each higher than the last to afford a clear view. Already they were filling up, ladies and gentlemen in elaborate hats and periwigs jostling for position.

The boxes loomed above, flanking the stage, dressed in bands of gilt leather. Here and there, a lady's fan shimmered in candlelight, or a powdered face leaned out to survey the crowd below.

At the far end stood the stage itself, jutting forward from a vast proscenium arch hung with heavy drapes, and lit around its perimeter with so many candles. Never had he witnessed such a magnificent arena. Not even the tiltyard in Whitehall was...

"Jacob!"

Pepys's tone snapped him from his reverie.

Ahead was a bottleneck of people, some heading upstairs to the right, others pressing toward the entrance to the pit. An attendant at each point was collecting fares, slowing the already sluggish mass.

Fortunately taller than most, Jacob could see over the crowd and spotted his employer's green felt hat a few bodies away.

"Coming, sir!" he called, and began pushing through the throng.

By the time he caught up with Pepys at the end of the passageway, he found himself level with the stage. Allowing himself a quick glance back, he caught the full majesty of the tiered galleries rising behind him, dotted about with shifting people, their low murmur building.

He felt a tug on his coat sleeve.

Pepys was pointing to a curtained doorway just ahead. "The tiring-house," he murmured.

Jacob looked blank.

Pepys sighed. "The place to which the actors retire, prior to their performance."

"I see. And what is our plan, sir?"

The other side of the curtain, a short flight of steps led them up into the wings. It struck Jacob that he was now standing beside the actual stage at the King's Playhouse - treading the same boards as the great players of his age. If only he knew their names.

The stage to his left was hidden from the audience by drapes. To its rear, a pair of painted boards stood within grooves in the floor, forming a classical palace: marble columns, high steps, and fluted archways that appeared to recede into shadow. Beyond them stood a wooden wall, with a curtained doorway set into each wing - through one of which Pepys and Jacob now passed into the tiring-house.

Once inside, they spotted, set centrally in the far wall, the door that Matt Tibbet must have used earlier: the tiring-house door. Flanking it were five makeshift timber rooms - two on the left and three, side by side, on the right. Each had a plain door and no windows, save for the room at the far left, which bore a single shuttered one.

That would be Tresillion's, Pepys realised: the manager's office, and the only room accessed from the passage behind the tiring-house. The others were likely tiring-rooms, where the players dressed in their stage attire.

Two more rooms stood against the side walls of the tiring-house - one just ahead of Jacob and Pepys, the other opposite, where a large table stood and Tibbet was busy tinkering.

The table was strewn with props: a crown and sceptre, a wine jug flanked by silver goblets, a sword, a scroll tied with a red ribbon, and other items Jacob could not quite make out. Beneath it lay curious maritime paraphernalia:

an anchor and sea chest, a cutlass, coiled ropes and folded flags.

Pepys caught Jacob's puzzled gaze. "Props, no doubt, from the previous production - which I did attend," he told him loftily. "The Young Admiral. Such is the pace at which plays are performed here, and routinely discarded."

Ropes hung from a ceiling as high as any the inquisitor had seen. Craning his neck to glimpse the pulleys way up in the fly gallery made him feel dizzy.

The tiring-house buzzed with purpose. Tailors stitched bodices, powdered wigs and adjusted trailing sleeves; scene-men hoisted backdrops and pushed platforms into place; while players paced nervously, muttering lines to themselves - all in feverish preparation for the afternoon's performance.

Intent on their own devices, none, fortunately, had spotted the interlopers.

"Mr Tresillion told us…" Jacob said, *sotto voce*.

"Nought, Jacob," Pepys hissed. "He told us nought."

"He admitted no guilt."

"*Neither did he proclaim his innocence*. Thus must we make our own enquiries."

Just then, Tibbet picked up a handbell and rang it a few times. "One quarter hour, ladies and gents!"

Footsteps and chatter clattered and buzzed anew.

Folk in stage attire began appearing from the rooms against the rear wall, several emerging from the larger one beside Tresillion's office. Dressed as soldiers and gentlemen in the fashions of the day - Jacob eyed a couple of elegant French *justaucourts* with envy - some gossiped, while others seemed lost in contemplation.

From the three adjacent tiring-rooms, a man stepped through the central doorway. He wore a rich burgundy doublet with slashed sleeves, a lace cravat, silk breeches and high leather boots, with a sword at his side. He carried himself with a swagger, nose lofted, arms swinging gaily, as if he had not a care in the world.

"Mr Lucius!" Pepys called, raising a finger. "Mr Lucius!"

Lucius stopped, stroked his sculpted chin, and sauntered toward him.

"Dorian Lucius," Pepys muttered to Jacob from the corner of his mouth, "who makes the ladies go weak at the knees."

"Do I know you, sir?" Lucius asked Pepys, upon reaching him.

"Aye, sir, I am…"

"Pepys! Is it not? Samuel Pepys?" The actor's vivid blue eyes seemed almost angelic.

"Why… aye… indeed." Pepys blustered, flushing. "I am honoured that you would remember me. I…" He faltered. "I find your stage attire, sir… delightful!"

Lucius smiled, flashing uncommonly white teeth, and brushed languidly at a sleeve. "I may have to sell it, so impoverished does Tresillion keep us."

Jacob and Pepys shared a glance. Before either could speak, they were joined by an older man, in his forties, and a woman who appeared to glow.

She was a vision in blue velvet, the gown somehow both sombre and alluring. Her rich chestnut hair was arranged in a courtly style, held in place by a jewelled pin. Her high cheekbones and dainty chin lent her face the shape of a heart.

He sported a broad red sash across his breast, with an engraved sword and plumed hat. Like Lucius, he thrust himself upright, posturing like a peacock - though his skin was more ravaged and his countenance plainer, and Lucius would more likely win the hen.

"Peregrine Marwood!" Lucius boomed. "Are we prepared?"

Then he took the lady's hand and kissed it. "And Franny Jenkins, my sweet!" He sniffed theatrically at her bosom. "Is that rosewater I detect, a-tickling my nostrils?"

"Nay, kind sir," she replied with feigned coyness. "'Tis just…"

The little group's attention was drawn by the slam of the tiring-house door, and the appearance of a most arresting young man.

Franny sneered. "'Tis just something foul I sniffed out last month."

Lucius ignored her. "Young Puck!" he called out, and the lad bounded towards him.

"*His name's Pip*," Marwood muttered sourly, then caught Jacob gazing doe-eyed at Franny. "Hands off, you gormless young buck! She's Lucius's."

Jacob, who had been called "gormless" plenty of times but never "young buck", coughed to cover his embarrassment.

"You look cold," Franny told the arriving Pip. "And your costume is covered in dust again." She tutted, airily brushing some away.

The lad glowered at her and moved closer to Lucius. "My apologies, Mr Lucius. I fear I'm late."

Lucius shrugged.

Pip, too, was dressed as a soldier, a bag of street clothing slung over his shoulder, yet looked nothing like the part. So handsome and unblemished was he, so painstakingly fashioned by his maker, that he more resembled a prince than a pikeman. His jet-black hair was swept back and tied with a blue ribbon, and his lips bore a provocative pout.

Franny dug Marwood in the ribs. "By the by, I ain't Lucius's. Ain't nobody's but my own."

"'Tis not what I heard," Marwood chimed back.

Retaking Franny's hand, Lucius leaned in and pecked her on the cheek. "And I assure you," he told Marwood, straightening with a wink, "you heard wrong."

Pip, watching on awkwardly, bowed. "I must apply my moustache," he said, and set off toward the largest of the tiring-rooms.

"He requires a fake one," Marwood muttered, "since he could not grow one himself, were he to live to a hundred."

Lucius grabbed his cheek and shook it, as if he were a child. "Are you jealous, Peregrine?"

Marwood slapped his hand away. "I am jealous of no man." He turned on Franny. "Nor you, hussy. Not long ago, you were barred from the boards. How I ache for the return of those days."

Lucius smirked. "You old curmudgeon, Peregrine. If only your adoring audience knew." Before Marwood could respond, he added, "By the by, where is Faybourne? He…"

"The idle coxcomb," said Marwood. "If only *his* audience knew the half of it. A more grotesque comic would be hard to find."

"I heard that!" came the curt reply, from the direction of the three adjacent tiring-rooms.

"And I second it!" added Lucius.

At that moment, the tiring-house door opened once again, and Thomas Tresillion appeared. Spying Pepys, he growled like a cornered animal and yelled across the room, "I told you to leave, Pepys! This is my theatre, not yours!"

Reddening, Pepys pushed at Jacob's chest, bundling him back towards the auditorium.

Behind them, they heard Dorian Lucius call out, "Farewell, Mr Pepys! I pray we meet again soon!"

"Count on it," Pepys muttered.

Chapter Eight

Orange Bess

Pepys and Jacob were squeezed onto the very end of one of the pit benches farthest from the stage. The attendant had assured Pepys the benches were full, until slipped an extra shilling - on top of the six for the seats - when space miraculously became available.

Unfortunately, nobody appeared to have told the lady to Pepys's left, who had to be cajoled then shunted aside, to unholy protests from both her and her husband (a prim fellow with a lisp).

Not that anybody took the blindest notice of the affray.

Jacob was still rather taken by his meeting with the cream of the King's Company. "I had no idea that actors were so marvellously handsome," he told Pepys.

"I have rehearsed the occasional scene myself, Jacob," Pepys replied, primping his periwig. "And I have dreamed of taking to the stage, for it becomes me. However…"

Jacob nodded slowly.

Pepys looked him up and down. "Indeed what, Mr Standish?"

The inquisitor froze. "Indeed… you would make a fine actor, sir."

Sniffing, Pepys nodded solemnly.

The auditorium was a riot of noise: hollers, barks, guffaws and screeches. Several gentlemen were on their feet, shouting across the pit to one another. Half a dozen young "orange girls", as Pepys referred to them, could be seen weaving their way among the seats and benches, selling fruit from baskets hung around their necks.

Their wares, it became apparent, were not always purchased for consumption. Jacob saw one half-eaten apple tossed into the lower gallery, only for it to come sailing back, narrowly missing his hat.

"Is it always like this?" he asked Pepys. "It feels more like a bawdy alehouse than a theatre."

Pepys clasped his hands together. "'Tis all part of the experience, Jacob. Does it not delight you? Here we are, witness to citizens from every crevice and corner of London." He turned. "Look behind you. The first gallery, where the tradesmen sit, amusing themselves after a hard day's labour. And above them, the upper gallery, crammed with apprentices, servants and the lower sort, who have scraped together their pennies in the pursuit of diversion."

"Aye, sir, I…"

But Pepys was not finished. "And there," he said, wafting both hands at the boxes high up, "recline in splendour the upper sort - on occasion the King himself - paying homage to this most glorious branch of the Arts."

"And who sits here?"

"In the pit? Why, we do, Jacob. We do. The gentry, the critics, the scholars."

Jacob hardly counted himself among any of those, but felt gratified to be seen in such exalted company.

Perhaps, he wondered, his new profession - as inquisitor - lofted him to such ranks. After all, Sir William Penn had asked after their services. A knight of the realm, no less.

He smiled to himself, just as the gentleman in front let out a vibrant belch, causing his companions to waft expensively gloved hands before their noses.

Jacob had seen Matt Tibbet lighting candles on two-tiered candelabras on either side of the apron stage. These were now being hauled on pulleys up toward the ceiling.

As the inquisitor followed their ascent, his eyes drifted to the lantern cupola he had seen from outside.

"Is that… rain entering the theatre?" he asked Pepys.

Pepys sighed. "Aye, Jacob, 'tis open to the elements up there. Admirable in the summer, less so in the winter. Grand as this playhouse may be, it has its faults. The passageways are too narrow, and the musicians are secreted 'neath the apron, which muffles the bass notes. I dare say they cannot be heard from the upper gallery. Not that I would deign to sit there."

As he spoke, a chorus of viols struck up, slow and stately at first, then, joined by flageolet and lute, building to a brisk allegro. Heads turned, and at least some of the audience hushed their chatter.

Standing, Jacob spotted the flash of sawing bows amid a group of dimly lit figures seated below the stage, just as Pepys had said. He had witnessed musical performance before, naturally, but this - this charged mix of tension, disorder and beauty - was something new.

"Sammy Pepys! You're never away from this place! You should set up a bed here. Mayhap I'll join yer." This was followed by a raucous laugh that dissolved into a hacking cough.

Retaking his seat, Jacob found an old woman standing beside his employer. She was dressed rather provocatively for her age, wearing a low-cut brocade bodice, with a fruit-filled apron at her waist. Her expression said, *I'll eat you alive.*

"This is Orange Bess," Pepys told Jacob. "Bess, may I present my personal inquisitor, Mr Jacob Standish?"

"Oooh!" said Bess, affecting a curtsey that cracked her joints. "Can I take him home with me? I'd rest his cheek on my bosom and feed him my oranges till the sun rose."

Pepys nudged his inquisitor. "A tempting invitation, is it not, Jacob?"

"Well, um, aye, indeed," Jacob managed. "I am… partial to an orange."

"I'm jesting with you!" Bess exclaimed, shoving him briskly in the chest. Unfortunately, he was unprepared and toppled backwards off the bench.

Suddenly, all around him - even those in the front rows of the gallery above - were on their feet, pointing, hooting and braying.

"Put him on the stage, for Heaven's sake!" he heard, as he regained his composure. "The man's funnier than Faybourne!"

The next he knew, arms were grabbing each of his limbs, and he was being hoisted towards the stage. He squirmed and struggled, but they could not be shaken off.

"Mr Pepys!" he cried out, craning his neck to see Pepys and Orange Bess cackling.

Chapter Nine

The Comic

Deposited unceremoniously on the stage, all Jacob could hear as he pushed himself to his feet was a wall of catcalls and hilarity. Looking out, he saw hundreds of pale faces, all fixed on him, mouths jabbering, as some pointed and others rocked in their seats.

"Name?" a voice below him demanded.

There, elbow resting louchely on the front of the stage, was a stick-thin man in a long powdered white periwig, all lace and buck teeth.

"Name?" the fop repeated.

"J-Jacob," Jacob stammered, bewildered, shrinking from the audience. "Jacob Standish."

The fop turned to address the house. "Ladies and gentlemen, Mr Jacob Standish!" He wafted an arm in the inquisitor's direction. "All the talent of dung – and the heart of a radish!"

A chorus of heckles rang out.

The fop only bowed, continuing with gusto.

"His performance resounds, like the bells of Shored-
itch.
Is that jaundice I've caught, or doth thrush make me
itch?
No meeting of minds, more a clash of his brows,
his presence onstage hath the grace of a cow!"

"You're the worst critic in all England, Edward
Eversley!" someone called out, to a roar of assent.
"Get him off!" bellowed another, and Jacob seized
the opportunity to slide offstage into the pit.
Every eye followed his progress as, ducking, he
skirted the benches apace to retake his seat.

His temples were throbbing, and his face burned as
he threw himself down beside Pepys.
"May we leave?" he whispered.
"Such foolish words," Pepys replied, his own cheeks
flushed red from so much laughter. "The performance
has yet to begin."
"But I…"
"Your antics will soon be forgotten, concern yourself not, Jacob. Such is the variety - and spice - of the
theatre."
"And Orange Bess?" Jacob asked, glancing about
nervously.

"You are safe from her clutches." Pepys patted his inquisitor's knee. "For the present."

The drapes parted, revealing a man in a brocade waistcoat strained at the buttons, bowing and scraping as he stepped forward. He wore a plum-coloured periwig, and a neat brown beard masked the curve of his jowls.

"Hugh Faybourne," Pepys muttered to Jacob. "The company's comic."

Faybourne stood there, milking the applause, exaggeratedly mopping his brow with a silk handkerchief. He remained that way for a good while, acknowledging various members of the audience with a nod or mouthed greeting, until a semblance of hush descended.

It was broken by a cry from the galleries. "Say it!"

That was followed by a chorus: "Aye! Say it!"

Faybourne cupped an ear. "What implore thee, pray? I cannot hear. Curse this damned spot in my ear."

They roared with laughter.

Pepys, noticeably, did not join in. "The man is witless," he told Jacob. "Yet they adore him."

Another voice rose above the clamour. "Say it!"

Faybourne dabbed his nose with the handkerchief, smiled, and bowed.

When he straightened, it seemed as if the entire crowd held its breath.

The comic threw open his arms. "'Twas not I!"

The place *erupted*.

Pepys buried his head in his hands.

Once the din had died down - interrupted by several choruses of "'Twas not I!" - Faybourne spoke again, feet planted firmly apart. "'Tis I the King's Company have called upon, to introduce to you our *petite* diversion, known to the common man - aye, I see you there, sir - as The Maid's Tragedy."

He paused, as so many folk wiped tears of mirth from glistening eyes. "However… I find I am having my hair trimmed."

With that, he flounced back through the drapes, leaving joyous uproar in his wake.

Chapter Ten

The Tragedy

The musicians' overture reached a crescendo, and the drapes parted to reveal a lavish backdrop: a courtly interior with classical columns lining the wings. Before it stood a cushioned bench, and four actors garbed in appropriate finery.

Wild cheers, without prompting, fell to an expectant hush.

"Who are these men?" Jacob asked.

Pepys, familiar with The Maid's Tragedy, leaned in to explain. "They are Lysippus, the King's brother, and two gentlemen of the court, Cleon and Strato - each in the hands of second-rate players." He pointed out an actor sporting a hat with a single feather and a sword at his hip. "That is the soldier, Diphilus, played there by young Pip Tredwell, whom we encountered earlier. He is making a name for himself upon the stage - whilst provoking jealousy among certain members of the company."

Cleon: The rest are making ready, sir.

Lysippus: So let them - there's time enough.

Diphilus: You are the brother to the King, my lord. We'll take your word.

Lysippus: Strato, thou hast some skill in poetry. What think'st thou of the masque? Will it be well?

Strato: As well as masque can be.

Lysippus: As masque can be?

Strato: Aye. They must commend their King and speak in praise of the Assembly; bless the bride and bridegroom, in person of some God. They're tied to rules of flattery.

Cleon: See, good my Lord, who is return'd!

When Peregrine Marwood strode onto the stage, re-splendent in sash and sword - somewhat longer than Diphilus's - spontaneous applause broke out. The critic, Edward Eversleigh, still standing at the front, slapped the stage with both hands.

"Bravo, sir!" he cried, before the actor had uttered a word.

Such was the commotion that Lysippus's next speech was all but drowned out.

Pepys turned to his inquisitor. "Melantius - the pillar of the piece. Mr Marwood is perhaps the finest actor of the age."

The gentleman in front, who had clearly overheard, swivelled sharply. "Nay, sir, that honour lies with Mr

Lansmere of the Duke's Company. Marwood's not fit to swill out his bedpan."

Before Pepys had a chance to reply, a booming, actorly voice rolled out across the auditorium, silencing the house once again.

Melantius: My lord, my thanks; but these scratch'd limbs of mine have spoke my love and truth unto my friends more than my tongue e'er could. My mind's the same - it ever was to you. Where I find worth, I love the keeper, till he let it go… and then I follow it.

…Accompanied by much gesticulation and clenching of the jaw.

Jacob was beginning to wish he had obliged Abby to attend in his place. Plays, he was quickly realising, were not his thing.

Some while later - it felt like an age to him, though was little more than a quarter-hour - Melantius concluded a speech to Dorian Lucius, whose first entrance as Amintor had caused a lady to swoon and be dragged from the pit.

The players retreated from the apron. The drapes were drawn closed, and the musicians struck up a sprightly air.

Jacob rose, stretched his arms, and yawned. "A fine play, sir," he said, hoping it sounded sincere. "Shall we adjourn to a tavern?"

Pepys stared up at his inquisitor, nonplussed. "'Tis not the end of the play, merely the end of the first act."

Jacob's mouth fell open. "The first act? There are more… acts?"

"Aye, Jacob," Pepys replied, uncertain whether his inquisitor was jesting. "There are five."

Jacob slumped back down. *Five?* he mouthed to himself.

"Did you not enjoy the first?" Pepys asked.

"I cannot swear to have understood it, sir."

Pepys sighed. "Amintor was meant to wed Aspatia, but the King insisted he take Evadne instead. Melantius has returned from war to honour the match, only to find his sister is now the bride, and Aspatia discarded. There is talk of a masque - but," he rubbed his hands with glee, "all is not as it seems."

"Indeed. We are yet to see the serving wench of the title."

Pepys curled his upper lip. "Serving wench?"

"The maid, sir, as noted in The Maid's Tragedy."

Pepys let out a strangled cough, as did the gentleman in front - wearing an annoyingly tall hat - who turned and pointed.

Jacob glared at him. "It would oblige me, sir, if you refrained from eavesdropping on our private discourse."

The gent nudged his neighbour. "This fopdoodle thinks the maid's a serving girl!" And together they descended into giggles.

"Ignore him, Mr Standish," said Pepys. "The play was published in the earlier part of the century. The 'maid' in question refers not to a servant, but to a chaste lady."

For the second time that afternoon, Jacob wished the ground would swallow him whole.

From behind the closed drapes came the sounds of shifting scenery, and when they parted, a velvet-clad throne now occupied the stage, flanked by regal banners.

Act II opened - to near-unanimous frothing - on Hugh Faybourne as the cantankerous Calianax, his long hair whitened, and his bulbous figure clad in a billowing gilded robe. It also introduced Franny Jenkins, playing the comely Evadne. She, above all the men, received the most ardent welcome.

Franny, Pepys informed Jacob, had been born into poverty and once sold fruit in theatres to survive. She had been plucked from obscurity by one of her managers and encouraged to act.

Prior to the King's return from exile, Pepys explained, women had been barred from the stage and all female roles played by men. However, Charles had encouraged - for reasons all too obvious - the employment of actresses. By now, it was frowned upon to have men playing women's roles.

Fascinating as such details were, by Act IV Jacob was fearful of falling asleep and toppling backwards off his bench again. The critic, Eversleigh, had not moved from his spot, and he did not wish to be paraded before the baying crowd once more.

In truth, he was more readily diverted by the audience than by the play.

Every time the Machiavellian King appeared onstage, bending others to his lustful will, an old woman among the front rows would rise and rebuke him, as if he were real. Urged to retake her seat by those behind, she sparked fisticuffs at one stage, which the actors ignored with apparent ease.

A pair of fops began loudly arguing over a lady; detritus - mostly fruit, though Jacob swore he spotted a sheep's eyeball - routinely rained down from the upper gallery; and more than once did somebody try to engage an emoting actor in conversation.

All the while, Eversleigh pronounced judgement on the performances, which the actors clearly found harder to ignore. When Hugh Faybourne's Calianax drifted suspiciously far from a contretemps centre-stage and trod on Eversleigh's hand, it did not look like an accident. (His improvised "'Twas not I!" rather gave the game away.)

The crowd surely lapped up the moment.

As the drapes closed on the fourth act, a pair of dancers skipped onto the apron to begin a rural frolic accompanied by lutes. He wore colourful silks, she ribbons and bells, and certain of the comments directed at them made Jacob blush.

Pepys puffed out his chest. On the whole, he said, the company was holding its own, requiring minimal prompting. "Although the overwrought fellow playing the King seems to think he is playing Lear."

Jacob had no idea what he meant, and decided it best not to ask.

Pepys reserved his most fulsome praise for young Pip. "He reminds me of Marwood at the same age. Such poise, such dignity, such timbre! How clearly I remember Peregrine portraying the Boy in Harry the Fifth."

And suddenly he was off his seat and quoting again.

"'They will steal anything and call it purchase. Bardolph stole a lute-case, bore it twelve leagues, and sold it for three halfpence.'" He all but bowed. "I knew then he was destined for greatness."

"Shut your cakehole!" the gentleman in front barked. "Pompous shot-clog."

Pepys pursed his lips. "How dare you address me in such a manner! I am Clerk of the Acts to the King's navy."

"Aye, and I'm its master shipbuilder."

Pepys was about to confront the fellow when Jacob ushered him back to his seat.

"Ignore the oaf, sir," Jacob said, aware it would be he doing any punching.

Act V – the final act, and Jacob had been counting – felt interminable, yet eventually all the chest-beating and pontificating seemed to reach a head.

The final curtain surely beckoned.

The stage was set with chairs and a table bearing a carafe, goblet and a candlestick. The columns remained but the banners were gone, and certain candles had been extinguished, lending the space a more foreboding atmosphere.

All the principal actors were present, most as background figures, with Lucius's Amintor and Franny's Evadne, the cursed husband and wife, centre-stage.

Evadne had slain the King, with whom she had been conducting an undesired affair, hoping it would win back her true husband, Amintor. At least, that was how Jacob saw it.

She clutched a dagger, her hands bloodied. They glared at one other with a fiery passion, Evadne's riven with desperation, his with confusion and ire.

Amintor: You now are present, stain'd with a king's blood, violently shed. This keeps night here, and throws an unknown wilderness about me… No more! Pursue me not!

Evadne: Forgive me then, and take me to thy bed. We may not part.

Amintor: Forbear! Be wise, and let my rage go this way.

Evadne [falling to her knees]: 'Tis you that I would stay, not it.

Amintor: Take heed, it will return with me.

Evadne: If it must be, I shall not fear to meet it. Take me home!

Amintor: Thou monster of cruelty, forbear!

Evadne: For Heaven's sake, look more calm. Thine eyes are sharper than thou canst make thy sword.

Amintor: Away, away! Thy knees are more to me than violence. I am worse than sick to see knees follow me, for that I must not grant. For Heaven's sake, stand.

"He means he cannot bear to see her grovel," Pepys hissed to Jacob, sensing his inquisitor's confusion.

Franny, dressed in a sombre, high-waisted gown, rose slowly to her feet. Her movement, elegant and studied, was mesmerising.

Jacob, finally, was rapt.

Evadne: Receive me, then.

Amintor: I dare not stay thy language. In midst of all my anger and my grief, thou dost awake something that troubles me and says, "I loved thee once." I dare not stay. There is no end of woman's reasoning.

As Lucius turned from her and strode to the wing, sword swaying at his side, Franny rushed to the table. She snatched up a goblet, drained it in one, then turned the dagger on herself, the tip hovering at her heart.

A collective gasp rose.

Jacob realised he was gripping Pepys's knee and snatched his hand away, mortified.

The entire auditorium held its breath, the only sound the shuffling of backsides in their seats. The background players inched forward, drawn inexorably toward the central pair, silent witnesses to Evadne's shame.

A clatter broke the spell as a sword dropped to the floor.

Groans followed, and Pepys said quietly to Jacob, "There is always one."

Faybourne opened his mouth to exclaim, until Pip, beside him, threw a hand over the comic's mouth, just in time.

Franny and Lucius, consummate in their roles, batted not an eyelid.

Evadne: Amintor, thou shalt love me now again. Go! I am calm. Farewell, and peace for ever! Evadne, whom thou hat'st…

Franny faltered, blinking furiously.

Evadne: …whom thou hat'st…

Throwing a hand to her mouth, she let her arms fall and sank to her knees.

Lucius stood tall. "…Will die for thee," he prompted.

Franny gazed up at him pleadingly, as a strangled gargling sound escaped her throat. "Will die…"

The audience craned forward in their seats to witness the tragic scene.

Franny's dagger slipped from her hand, something beyond fear etched on her face.

"… for thee," she gasped, then toppled forward, flat on her face.

The house rose as one, a delirium of congratulation and applause.

"Bravo!" so many cried. "Bravo!"

The cast stood around Franny's unmoving body, glancing nervously from one to the other.

Lucius dropped to the floor, turned her over, and cradled her head in his lap, concern etched on his smooth face.

"Franny?" He slapped her cheek, and her head flopped to the side. "Franny!" More urgent now.

His fellow players edged closer.

"Was she not supposed to stab herself?" Edward Eversleigh wondered aloud.

In that instant, the mood shifted. The applause thinned to a ripple, and a rumble of unease began to spread.

From one of the wings, Matt Tibbet rushed onstage, snatched up the goblet Franny had drunk from and peered inside. Wiping a finger around the inner rim, he extracted a sludgy white residue and sniffed at it.

Pepys and Jacob cast each other a glance.

When Pepys nodded, Jacob hurried forward, his employer close behind.

Extending a yellowed tongue, Tibbet took a cautious lick of the sludge.

His features twisted and he wiped a sleeve across his mouth. "Poison!"

Lucius, still kneeling, clasping the lifeless Franny to his chest, and wailed to the rafters, "Nay!"

All hell broke loose.

There were so many bodies on the stage, bustling like panicked ants, some weeping, others merely enjoying the sensation. By the time Jacob and Pepys arrived, that they had to force their way through to Tibbet.

"Where is the goblet?" Jacob demanded.

Wordlessly, dazed, Tibbet handed it over.

Dipping a fingertip into the white sludge, Jacob raised it to his mouth and licked. It tasted bitter, and burned his tongue. Nodding to himself as Pepys and Tibbet watched on, he raised the vessel to his eyeline and twisted it in his fingers, inspecting every facet.

The goblet was silver, its bowl decorated with acanthus leaves and mounted on a knobbed stem. Beneath the rim, in white enamel, was a horizontal white bar from which three rectangular pendants dropped, each bearing three red roundels.

Pepys pointed at it. "How do you explain this?" he asked Tibbet.

Tibbet's pale scar seemed throb, but his tongue would not move.

Jacob squinted. "What is it, sir? What have you found?"

Pepys jabbed a finger at the enamel marking. "This is the Duke's label, Jacob, not the King's. Why is it here, Tibbet?"

Tibbet had no answer.

Jacob spoke up. "Then this goblet, which poisoned the poor lady, likely came from the Duke's Company." He turned to Pepys. "And who is in charge there, sir?"

"Mr Edmund Fletcher."

The inquisitor almost dropped the goblet. During their very first investigation, he had had the misfortune to visit the home of one Edmund Fletcher, a brute of a man, whose drawing-room walls had been lined with theatrical playbills… It all added up.

"The same man Abby is convinced started London's terrible fire?" he asked.

"I have heard it said," Pepys replied, "though I consider it the height of fancy."

Chapter Eleven

Edmund Fletcher

Faversham, Kent, 1635

On the pilgrim route into Canterbury lay the prosperous town of Faversham. Connected to London, some fifty miles distant, via Faversham Creek and the River Swale, it boasted Kent's oldest market, dating back beyond the Battle of Hastings, and once exported more wool than any other English port.

Its prominence was built on trade. Grain, oysters from the local fishery, gunpowder and hops moved to and from the town, enriching its more enterprising inhabitants.

One such gentleman was Giles Fletcher, whose granaries flanked the upper creek, and whose sloops bore his name. Three generations of Fletchers had traded grain from Faversham, and Giles had more than doubled the family's holdings. A God-fearing Protestant, he was not a man given to grand speeches, nor one who suffered trifles. The townsfolk bore him respect, which pleased him.

His family estate, Elmleigh House, stood on a rise beyond Abbey Fields. It allowed Giles a view across the marshes and tidal waters of the Swale, and he would often gaze from an upstairs window at the never-ending flow of trade. Movement meant money, and money meant the world.

Giles's wife, Agatha, gave him two sons: Nathaniel and Edmund. Nathaniel, the elder, died of a fever in 1633, aged thirteen. Marked out to inherit the family business, his death sewed panic and confusion. Agatha wore her grief like a suit of armour; Giles feared the wrong son had survived.

Edmund was a dissolute sort – defiant, restless and brash, with his head forever in the clouds. He had been dismissed from the local grammar school for insolence, and wore the badge with pride, which only deepened his parents' dismay.

He had no interest in the grain trade, which he made abundantly clear. Were Elmleigh House not set apart from the town, the local gossips would surely have revelled in the sounds of Giles's raging, and his son's unflinching rebuttals.

Some wondered why Giles did not disown the lad. In truth, he had little choice but to do battle.

And what a battle it became.

Not long after his brother died, Edmund was charged with accompanying old Jonas Kettley, his father's most trusted barge captain, on a delivery run to London. He was to hand a ledger to one of the city's grain agents and return with a signed receipt.

One of Giles's pet greyhounds could have achieved the tasks - but not Edmund.

The moment the barge docked at Queenhithe, he was off, minus the ledger, Kettley's despairing cries in his wake. Here, he decided, was the chance to explore, a freedom long denied him under his father's watchful eye. Faversham felt so stifling; in London, Edmund sensed opportunity.

He quickly became lost in its thronged maze of centuries-old streets, gazing up and around, mouth agog and eyes wild. The noise was constant, the odours drifting from the cookshops alluring. Each new street exuded a desire for life and livelihood, and people fired with purpose barged him rudely aside. He only marvelled.

Reaching St Paul's Churchyard, in the shadow of the vast cathedral - so towering and grand, yet streaked with soot and filth - he browsed the booksellers' stalls, picking up books and broadsides. He could read well enough, and it was words he desired, not his father's precious numbers.

At length, he found himself in a shabby court off Drury Lane, at a tall, timber-framed, whitewashed building with a steep, gabled roof. Around it were taverns, tenements and stables. While the smell of the horses was familiar to him, so much else was not.

A young woman with a crafty smile and heaving bosom sidled up beside him. "You lost, young master? Why don't I show you a play more daring that anything you'll find in there?

Hmm?" Gesturing to the tall building opposite, she raised a teasing eyebrow.

Edmund grimaced. "What is that place?"

The woman performed a double-take. "You really are lost, ain't yer? That's the famous Cockpit theatre, my sweet. Now, why don't yer hand Gertie some coin an' we'll see where the mood takes us?" She rubbed the collar of his velvet coat between a grubby thumb and forefinger. "Looks like yer father's worth a tidy sum. How much d'he give yer?"

Edmund slapped her hand away. "How dare you, brazen wench!" he snapped. "My father gives me nought. And if I had money, I would certainly not hand it to you!"

He turned away, and she took the opportunity to kick him up the backside, to the jeers and delight of several onlookers.

"Pompous little popinjay!" she mocked.

Stung, yet suddenly fearful, he hurried into the knot of people outside the Cockpit, ducking among the clustered bodies.

"A penny," said the man at the door, proffering a palm.

As Edmund had informed that uncouth young woman, he had no money, not even a penny. His father did not trust him with coin.

A surge in the crowd behind jolted him forward, and he simply let the motion carry him, darting through the entrance while the doorman only sighed. He could live without the penny. The place was filling fast, and turned a sizeable profit.

Edmund found himself in the pit, staring in wonder as the world and his wife bustled past to secure a space on the benches. So many people – a barrage of chatter – up there in the galleries, their lively features illuminated by a blaze of candlelight, intent upon the wide stage with its painted blue ceiling. Musicians were tuning lutes and viols in a gallery off to one side. The odours of tallow, tobacco and sweat assaulted his nostrils as his other senses became gloriously overwhelmed.

He had heard of theatres, naturally, but his father was not one to entertain such fripperies. Now he was inside one, and it dazzled him. The experience felt like… all he could compare it with was church. The space, the people, rich and poor, clerk and cutpurse. But this – this felt forbidden. It felt wrong.

Yet so right.

And then the play started!

When Edmund left the Cockpit that afternoon, his young mind had burst open.

The poetry, the elegance – the madness! – of what he had just experienced felt shocking.

The play, he later learned, was The Changeling.

A young woman, Beatrice-Joanna, had first taken the stage. Wilful and devious, she had rejected her father's preferred suitor in favour of her own – just as Edmund rejected the career his father had laid out for him. Powdered and rouged, she wore a gown of the finest materials and spoke in soft, lilting tones, yet… It had taken Edmund a while to realise the actor was a boy, like himself.

Never had he witnessed anything like it.

The self-absorbed youth saw his own life mirrored up there. The production spoke to him, it whispered truths in his ear. Are all plays like this? he wondered, discovering for the first time the anarchic and compelling resonance of Art.

Might he become a theatrical player?

It would send his father into apoplexy!

Every dastardly urge of mankind had been portrayed inside the Cockpit that day – lust, betrayal, corruption, murder, and so many more – each writ large upon the wooden stage, garbed in velvet, ruffs and silk, enunciated with passion and venom.

How it fired him.

However, though Edmund Fletcher returned from London with his head in the clouds, his feet remained firmly wedged in his father's house. And Giles would hear none of the lad's nonsense.

When Edmund suggested forming a band of local players to stage performances at the town's guildhall, his father laughed until he feared his breeches would burst open, then thrashed the boy to drive out the devilry.

Edmund pleaded for the money to buy broadsides from the stationer's stall at the market, and was told he had not earned it. Even when he toiled despite himself at the company's ledgers, he was denied his wage.

"Your reward shall come when you inherit all I've built, and not a moment before," Giles told him. "Only then will you understand the value of grain and toil, and 'twill make a man of you."

Edmund was trapped.

And so he plotted.

Every year, the Fletchers held a midsummer feast on their estate, welcoming buyers, trading partners and local dignitaries: aldermen, clergy, merchants and magistrates. Everyone in the town hoped for an invitation.

When the weather held, the event took place outdoors on one of the lawns. Tables groaned under the weight of food, a whole ox was roasted, wine and beer flowed freely, and a single viol player strummed innocuously in the background.

Giles hosted in his most ostentatious ruff, wheeling between guests, patting his great stomach while Agatha trailed in his wake, simpering. Both were far too busy to notice that Edmund was nowhere to be seen.

The first they became aware of him was when he announced, over the clamour of the party, "Pray, silence! I beg your ears for the tragedy about to unfold!"

That took their attention.

Edmund had hung one of the family tapestries – a bucolic farming scene – between two trees at the edge of the adjacent orchard, and had commandeered the musician to accompany him on lute.

Dressed in his clerk's attire, he had chalked his face white and had painted a single black tear on his cheek.

With a flourish, he bowed. "I present to you: The Martyr of Elmleigh! A tale no man but I dare tell!"

Nodding to the bemused musician to begin playing, he lofted one of his father's leather-bound ledgers high into the air, mopping his brow in theatrical despair.

The guests fell silent, caught between staring at Edmund and at his outraged parents, who had become rooted to the spot in abject horror.

"O ledger, thou cold and callous tome!
Thine ink doth bleed upon my soul.
A tally of my bondage."

Edmund caught his father's low growl, but pressed on.

"Must I be bound like ox to plough?
When thoughts of Art within this brow,
suffuse my waking dreams?"

He dropped to his knees, clutching the ledger to his chest, addressing the heavens.

"Deny me not, cruel hand of fate!
Is this family name my gallows?
Let me rise – aye, rise! – upon this stage!

I, Edmund! The Martyr of Elmleigh."

A murmur of shock swept the onlookers, until Giles, dis-covering his senses, strode forward, vengeance on his mind. However, a few mischievous folk halted his progress, urging him to let the lad be.

It worked, for a while, until Edmund, who had retired behind the tapestry, reemerged wearing his mother's coat and hat.

Like Fire

The King's Company sought sanctity in the tiring-house, while flustered attendants scrambled to usher people out. The narrow passageways, prone to bottlenecks, only made matters worse.

Yet even the tiring-house was a scene of fluster and confusion. People wept openly, and Jacob could scarce distinguish theatre folk from the invading audience. He spotted Eversleigh, loudly proclaiming a curse upon the King's Company, while others berated him and a few nodded sagely.

Tibbet cleared the props table with the sweep of an arm, and Lucius set Franny down. The fear trapped in her eyes was unnerving, and he gently closed her eyelids.

Her pale lips were blistered.

Dorian Lucius looked fit to weep - but then he was a fine actor, Jacob mused. Perhaps the finest of his age.

Peregrine Marwood stood grim-faced, while Hugh Faybourne toyed idly with a button on his waistcoat.

Pepys, nudging Jacob forward, spoke up. "Gentlemen, I have yet been unable to introduce you to my personal inquisitor, Mr Jacob Standish."

Jacob, reaching instinctively for his periwig, bowed.

"If there is a murderer in our midst – and it seems certain there is – then he will surely root out the devil. I, Samuel Pepys, give you my word."

Faybourne tutted, and Lucius glared at him.

Jacob cleared his throat. "Mr Trippet…"

"*Tibbet!*" Tibbet barked.

Marwood raised an eyebrow. "He's funnier than you, Faybourne."

"I–I do beg your pardon, Mr Tibbet…" Jacob hesitated. "Pray, what is your function here?"

Tibbet narrowed his eyes. "I don't answer to you. I answer only to Mr Tres…"

"He's the stagekeeper," Lucius cut in. "Jack of all trades." His eyes flicked to the poisoned goblet beside its victim. "Also in charge of the props."

Tibbet moved to confront him, thick fists clenched.

Lucius, grinning fearfully, took a few steps back. "Must I remind you, Tibbet, that 'tis I who fills the company purse? Lay one filthy digit on me and Tresillion will have you out the door faster than Hugh here can clear an auditorium."

Faybourne snorted. "Remember The Duchess of Malfi, Dorian?"

"I was handed the part only the night before," Lucius replied indignantly, "since…"

Pepys raised his arms. "Gentlemen! I beseech you, have some decorum. A lady lies dead."

"Who did you say you were?" Peregrine Marwood asked Pepys.

"He's Samuel Pepys," said Lucius.

"Clerk of the Acts to the Navy Board," Jacob added.

"Then what in the blazes is he doing here?" Marwood snapped and turned on his heel. "You have no place here, sir."

They were getting nowhere.

Pepys looked imploringly to Jacob.

The inquisitor had had his fill of actors, yet his duty lay with Pepys.

Were Abby with him, she would have stepped in, and - too often, he realised - he allowed it.

Straightening his coat, he picked up the goblet. "This poison…"

"Corrosive sublimate," Tibbet cut in. "Seen it before. Ships' barber-surgeons use it to cure the pox."

"You have some in your possession?"

Tibbet paused. "I do not."

"And you served…?"

"First mate on the Swan."

"Aye, Mr Tibbet, you have the look of a sailor." Jacob had had his fill of sailors, too. "You made straight for this poisoned goblet, as I recall?"

Tibbet jutted out his chin. "What you implyin'?"

"He implies, Matthew, that you murdered poor Franny," Lucius said. "Did she not lately… reject you?"

The stagekeeper sucked in a breath. "She did not. Malicious lies, such are traded with abandon in this place." A wry smile curled on his lips. "And what of you, Lucius? Were you not seen with her in a lovers' embrace only yesterday? All saw it."

"We were rehearsing a part!"

"Oh aye." Tibbet waggled his little finger, winking. "And which part would that be?"

Lucius snarled. "Even if we were lovers…"

"Did she not reject you also, Mr Lucius?" Jacob interjected. "She told us herself, as I recall it: 'I ain't Lucius's. Ain't nobody's but mine'."

Lucius glared at Jacob, and Pepys was once again obliged to appeal for calm. It having been restored, he motioned for Jacob to proceed.

"I wondered also," Jacob said, "what opportunity our murderer had to apply the poison to the goblet? Where was it kept, Mr Tibbet?"

"On this very table, where anybody might've tampered with it. I moved it to the stage 'twixt Acts IV and V. See here…" Tibbet bent down and retrieved a silver goblet from among the piled props on the floor. "There are others, but they were empty. I transferred the only full goblet."

"Which bore Duke of York's mark," Pepys pointed out.

But Jacob was no longer listening. His attention had been drawn elsewhere among the props, and he lifted out a silk handkerchief between thumb and forefinger.

"And 'tis monogrammed." He laid the embroidered initials in the palm of his hand. "H.F."

All eyes turned on Hugh Faybourne.

"What reason had you, sir, to visit this props table?" Jacob asked.

If he had hoped to intimidate the comic, he was much mistaken.

Faybourne sniffed. "'Twas not I," he quipped.

Lucius punched him full in the jaw, sending him sprawling to the floor.

For a large fellow, Faybourne was up quickly, and the two famed actors squared off, fists raised.

Lucius laughed. "How funny you look - for once."

"Faybourne!" came the bark. "Lucius! How dare you demean my theatre!"

Pepys and Jacob turned to see Thomas Tresillion striding towards them. Fearing the worst, Pepys lowered his head. As he did so, Tibbet slipped away.

Tresillion only rolled his eyes when he saw Pepys. Lucius and Faybourne dropped their fists and glared at one other. Jacob, meanwhile, was rooted to the spot, still holding out the monogrammed handkerchief.

"What is this?" Tresillion asked him.

"I… I found it, sir, among the props there." Jacob nodded toward the pile.

"What of it?"

"'Tis Mr Faybourne's, sir. We know not how it came to be there, alongside the poisoned goblet."

Tresillion turned to his comic. "Well?"

"I have dozens, Thomas. One may have become discarded. Or," he stared pointedly at Lucius, "it may have been planted, to draw attention from another's guilt."

"Why would I kill her?" Lucius spluttered.

"Since my audiences came to favour her over you?" said Tresillion.

Faybourne sniggered.

"And you, *comic*." Tresillion glared. Then he turned to the still form of Franny Jenkins, enchanting even in death, and sighed loudly. "I have spent the past quarter-hour consoling a succession of dukes and lords, each devastated by her demise. She kept commendable company."

Pepys coughed politely. "Mr Tresillion?"

"What is it, Pepys? I banished you from this tiring-house."

"I assure you, sir, my inquisitor and I seek only to assist in this dire matter. It did occur to me… We have heard motives of love and jealously, yet no one has thought to mention money. Did Mistress Jenkins hold shares in the King's Company? And in the event of her tragic death, might such shares be divided among the rest?"

The slight Tresillion, overwhelmed by his attire, seemed to rear up, nostrils flared. Enraged, with his skeletal features he appeared almost… demonic. Jacob swallowed, Pepys backed off; even the actors, surely well accustomed to Tresillion's rages, turned pale.

"I shall not discourse with outsiders on the subject of money!" the manager thundered. "'Tis a matter for myself and His Majesty alone. You do sorely test my patience, Pepys." He shook his head, as if contemplating treason. "Begone, sir, and take your… *inquisitor* with you. If I catch you in my tiring-house again, so help me God, I shall banish you from this theatre altogether."

Pepys's bulging eyes widened and he raised his hands in supplication. "I would not wish that, Mr Tresillion. You know how much I…"

Tresillion folded his arms. "Indeed I do, Pepys."

"Yet how can we bring to justice the foul demon who did…?"

"Heed my words, sir." Tresillion spoke deliberately. "I. Do. Not. Wish. For your service."

Pepys exhaled, defeated. "Come, Jacob."

As the pair headed for the door, they heard Tresillion discussing with Lucius and Faybourne the dire need for a new principal actress.

"Could Clara Lovick not take Franny's role?" said Faybourne.

"Then who would take Clara's?" Tresillion replied. "Anyhow, she is not up to it. Franny had them baying in their seats, she illuminated the stage with her presence. Did you see Mistress Lovick's Aspatia today? She bore all the melancholy of Falstaff. The house laughed when Amintor abandoned her."

Without warning, Pepys stopped. Nudging Jacob to follow, he retraced his steps.

Tresillion looked flabbergasted when Pepys reappeared. His actors squirmed with delight.

Pepys raised his hands in supplication. "Mr Tresillion, ere you speak, allow me the privilege, then I shall duly depart."

Tresillion silently raised his eyes to the heavens.

"I know of an actress, sir," Pepys went on, "who plays in the basement of a tavern near the Tower…"

"What is her name?" Tresillion asked.

"She moves with the grace of a sylph, sir, and is mighty handsome. Her Desdemona reduced grown men to tears. Myself, I confess, included."

Lucius, brightening, asked, "Handsome, you say?"

"Long hair like fire itself, Mr Lucius, and eyes of deepest turquoise."

Jacob choked.

"And what is her name, Pepys?" Tresillion demanded.

"Her name, sir, is Abigail Harcourt."

Chapter Thirteen

The Scrawled Hand

"*An actress?*" Abby sprang from her chair at Jacob's on Strand Lane. "But I can't act!"

Pepys chuckled. "Neither can half the players in London."

"At least they have stood upon a stage!" Her voice was shrill. "Sir, I've ne'er so much as seen a play!"

Pepys calmly laced his fingers together. "Yet you have read several, Abigail. Works by Mr Dryden, Mr Shirley, Mr Shakespeare…"

Abby began pacing, dragging her fingers through her hair. Her coif slipped off, and Jacob stopped to retrieve it.

She snatched it back with a murderous glance. "What shall I do?" she pleaded. "How shall I…"

"All this bluster is by the by, since the matter is settled. I had no choice, Abigail. Mr Tresillion banished myself and Jacob." Pepys slapped his hands on his knees. "We meet with him tomorrow at dawn, at Browne's Coffee House in Covent Garden."

Raising his stemmed glass of sack, enamelled with the Standish family crest, he took a delicate sip.

And that, Abby realised, was that.

There had been one further incident at the King's Playhouse, before Pepys and Jacob took their leave.

On passing through the tiring-house door, they were accosted in the passageway by Matt Tibbet, the stage-keeper. Pulling them into shadows, he thrust a roll of paper, bound around a slim dowel, into Pepys's hand.

"What is this?" Pepys asked.

"A cue roll," said Tibbet, motioning for him to read.

Shuffling nearer to an oil lamp, Pepys unrolled the paper. Inked lines from a play filled the narrow strip, with cues scrawled in the margins. "Somebody's part?"

Tibbet licked his flaking lips. "Aye. But whose?"

"'*Thou art Melantius'*,'" Pepys recited under his breath. "'*All love is spoke in that - a sacrifice to thank the Gods, Melantius is returned in safety.*' Why, these words are Amintor's. This is Lucius's part."

Tibbet leered. "Aye, Lucius." He spat on the floor. "Now scroll on."

As Pepys did so, rolling through the lines, the stage-keeper suddenly stayed his hand. "There!"

With a glance at his inquisitor, Pepys peered.

Reading over his shoulder, Jacob pointed. "Look, sir - a different hand."

Pepys scrolled through a few more feet of paper. Indeed, the wispy, pale writing appeared nowhere else. Feverishly, he rolled back to the irregular scrawl.

Remember I can help you sink him. Just say the word.

"'Remember I can help you sink him. Just say the word.'?" Pepys read aloud, then glanced up. "Sink whom?"

Tibbet snatched the roll back. "Mine," he snapped.

Jacob spoke up. "Where did you find that?"

"'E left it in the privy."

Pepys's face puckered. "*Dorian Lucius learns his lines in the privy?*"

Tibbet pushed an oily finger to Pepys's lips. "Hush!" he hissed. "Tell no one."

"Who wrote it?" Jacob asked. "And who do they mean to sink?"

Retrieving his finger, Tibbet wiped it on his jerkin, to Pepys's consternation. "Could be anyone. 'Es jealous of 'em all."

"*Dorian Lucius?*" Pepys spluttered. "*Jealous?*"

"Hush, I told yer!" Tibbet growled, baring teeth the colour of mud. Lowering his voice, he added, "Franny - 'e was jealous of 'er. 'Ow she wins the crowd with a toss of her curls. Faybourne…"

"*Jealous of…*" Jacob began, too loudly, and lowered his voice. "Jealous of Faybourne?"

"Aye, they love 'im, didn't yer hear? Clod as he may be. Lucius seethes with jealousy. Marwood upstages him, Lansmere, Franny…"

Jacob stopped him with a hand. "Lansmere?" It was a name he had not heard before.

"Benedict Lansmere," said Pepys. "Defected from the King's Company to the Duke's…" He paused.

"A year ago," Tibbet added, wistful. "Now there's a fine actor. And a gentleman. Treated me proper, he did. With respect. Not like this lot."

"And who wrote the note?" Jacob asked.

"Couldn't say for sure…" Tibbet left the words hanging.

Pepys sighed, fished for his purse and held out a penny. "Were you to hazard a guess?"

Tibbet bit the coin, and nodded. "I'd say 'twas Franny Jenkins's hand. Rumour holds, she returned here late one night, a month or two since, seeking a lost glove. Days later, Lansmere's gone. 'Tis said, she saw something. Something she could hold against him."

"Is it true? Who told this tale?"

Tibbet shrugged. "Tales in this place are stock in trade. Some true, most mere fancy."

"And whom do you believe murdered the woman?"

Tibbet pulled Pepys in close, clutched his ear, and whispered into it, "Orange Bess."

Pepys tutted. "I find that most unlikely."

Chapter Fourteen

Pepys's Desdemona

"Fortunately, I have a copy of this," said Pepys, handing Abby a dark, calfskin-bound quarto.

Opening it, she read aloud. "'The Tragedy of Othello, the Moor of Venice'? I know of it, but haven't read it."

"Then I suggest you do so, paying great attention to the part of Desdemona."

Abby looked at him quizzically.

Pepys cleared his throat. "Since I informed Thomas Tresillion, manager of the King's Playhouse, that your playing of the part reduced grown men to tears."

Abby's jaw dropped, and Pepys winced.

Outside, a drunken voice railed against injustice and a hound howled a lament.

Inside, the now-familiar faces of the Standish family gazed disapprovingly down from their portraits, as the flames in the hearth licked at the chimney's soot.

Abby had to compose herself. It would have been un-wise to launch a tirade at her former master. Only months ago, she had been his maidservant, lately promoted to inquisitor – a role that had freed her in so many ways. Not only from the drudgery and interminable hours, but also from a life in which her mind lay sluggish and idle. Now, she was allowed to think.

And she deserved it, she kept assuring herself.

Pepys took the quarto from Abby and flicked through the thick, yellowed pages. "Here, Act IV, Scene 3." He handed it back opened, pointing. "Read that."

"'My mother had a maid called Barbara. She was in love, and he she loved…'"

"Nay, nay, nay, Abigail. Play the part! Desdemona may be Shakespeare's most tragic heroine. She married Othello for love, infatuated. Yet he believes she has wronged him, lying with another man, and will take his revenge. Here, she senses it…"

Pepys stood before the chairs at the fire – an audience of two – imagining himself onstage at the King's Playhouse. Chest out, billowing cuffs flung wide, he began:

"My mother had a maid call'd Barbara:
She was in love; and he she loved proved mad
And did forsake her: she had a song of 'willow,'
An old thing 'twas, but it express'd her fortune,
And she died singing it: that song tonight
Will not go from my mind."

He sank, he rose, he beat on his chest and tore at his cheeks. His face flushed crimson, and his glinting brown eyes took on a haunted emptiness.

"Bravo!" Jacob cried when Pepys had finished, applauding like a man possessed.

When he had calmed down, Abby said drily, "You would make a marvellous Othello, sir."

He had shown her, at least, that the lady's role required subtlety.

Before she retired to her guest chamber with a stack of quartos, to prepare for the following day, Pepys and Jacob recounted their findings at the theatre.

They told of the note Tibbet had found, supposedly written by the murder victim to Dorian Lucius, whom rumour named as her paramour.

Remember I can help you sink him. Just say the word.

"To whom was it addressed?" Abby asked.

Pepys wrinkled his nose. "According to the stage-keeper, Tibbet, Lucius is jealous of the entire King's Company - and half of the Duke's. I find it barely credible. The fellow is a sly dog. I trust him not."

Abby looked to her fellow inquisitor for affirmation.

He could only shrug. "Tibbet claims Orange Bess is guilty."

"What think you?" she asked.

"I swear Marwood's hands looked white," he said. "The colour of the poison."

"Or pale with the cold?" Pepys added. "Or from some theatrical powder?"

Jacob spread his palms. "You must find more clues, Abby."

"But where should I look?"

Pepys slugged back his sack. "The actors may be a spiteful group, prone to envy and pride, yet they are surely too versed in the Arts to be capable of such a terrible crime."

As the church bells outside began chiming the eleventh hour, he stretched and yawned. "Do pardon me. The hour is late. Were I you, Abigail, I would turn my attentions to Thomas Tresillion. His office is in such disarray that I fear for his mind. Money lies at the heart of this matter, mark my words. Discover who holds shares in the King's Company, and who stands to gain by Franny's demise – then you shall find our murderer."

Undeterred, knowing Abby would wish to be prepared, Jacob described each of the principal actors and recalled, as best he could, their discourse.

He then relived the events of Franny Jenkins's death on stage. When he came to the poisoned goblet, he halted abruptly after describing its design - the Duke's label - and glanced at Pepys.

Both men were all too aware of Abby's obsession with Edmund Fletcher of the Duke's Company - and with his supposed assassin, Henry Trevelyan, whom the inquisitors knew as "Hook-Hand" for the hand he had lost in naval service.

She was convinced that Fletcher had hired Hook-Hand to intimidate the Baxters of Pudding Lane, fearing William Baxter possessed proof of his wife's infidelity and wanted it destroyed. In Abby's mind, that chain of events had led to Hook-Hand inadvertently starting the terrible fire that levelled the city the previous September.

"What is it?" she asked. "What was that look?"

Pepys sighed, drumming his fingers on the arm of his chair. "You know not who manages the Duke's Company?"

Warily, she looked from Pepys to Jacob.

Jacob swallowed. "Edmund Fletcher."

Abby had to be dissuaded from leaving Strand Lane that instant, to hammer on the door of the Duke's Playhouse.

"We have no proof of Fletcher's involvement, beyond a goblet bearing the Duke's mark," Pepys pointed out.

Abby shook her head in disbelief. "The goblet was poisoned!"

Pepys gulped some more sack. "Aye, but any man…"

"Or woman," Jacob interjected.

"…or woman might have transferred it to the King's theatre. Why, it may even have been stolen."

Abby rubbed her cheek.

Pepys continued, "Should you discover some proof of Mr Fletcher's involvement, then I shall permit you to investigate further. Until that time, I fear it would only muddy the waters. Hmm?"

He caught her gaze. "Have I made myself clear?" Satisfied that he had, he concluded, "You are an astute and prudent young woman, Abigail. That is why I assigned to you to this most troubling task. You shall, I am convinced, prevail, whence this foul devil who brings death to His Majesty's very theatre shall be unmasked."

Jacob's eyes lit up. "Sir?"

"What is it, Jacob?"

The inquisitor rubbed his hands together, grinning idiotically. "'Twas not I!"

A graveyard hush enveloped the room. Even the dogs outside ceased their howling.

"Mr Standish." Pepys stared down his nose. "Should you ever repeat that idiot phrase again, I shall drum you from my service."

Chapter Fifteen

Covent Garden

Abby slept not a wink, between thumbing through Pepys's printed plays by candlelight and fretting over her ability to pass herself off as a seasoned actor. She felt irritated that Pepys had forced her into the situation, yet also enlivened by the prospect of such glorious subterfuge.

As he had suggested, she dwelt longest on Othello, a play she had not read before. Shakespeare's language was so poetic that at times she found herself holding her breath. His themes struck a chord. How many devious, calculating Iagos had she encountered in recent months? And how keenly she felt Othello's torment - the burden of honour, the ache of doubt, the ease with which trust could be shattered.

She practised Desdemona's key lines, time and again, until the words came easily.

Mr Pepys was relying on her, she reminded herself.

"Did you sleep well?" Pepys asked, as Abby joined the two men for breakfast some while before dawn.

"Most soundly, sir," she chirped, surreptitiously rubbing a bleary eye.

Jacob's maid was not due, so he had raided the pantry for anything edible.

Pepys picked up the loaf, blinked, and tapped it on the table. It went *clonk*.

Turning it over in his hands, he discovered a small hole in one side and tore it in half with some difficulty. The loaf was hollow.

"It seems a mouse has beaten us to it," he said.

Horrified, Jacob grabbed a dish of cold bacon and pushed it across the table towards his employer. In doing so, he knocked over his mug of small ale, the pool of flat liquid heading rapidly in Pepys's direction.

Pepys leapt from his chair. "I find I am not hungry. The hour is too early for sustenance."

"I concur," said Abby, rising. "There's much to be done."

"Cheese?" Jacob offered weakly, proffering a lump of something yellow with bluish-green spots.

Pepys raised a firm hand. "I think not, Jacob."

They had become accustomed to the winter's insistent chill and were dressed against it.

The men wore hats, cravats, gloves and thick coats. Pepys's was lined with silk and padded with fur, considerably more expensive than Jacob's dour affair. But then, the inquisitor was not one to stand out in a crowd.

Abby had once again rifled through Jacob's sisters' wardrobes, and decided - to her chagrin - that Anne's flamboyant tastes might suit the occasion best. She paired white silk petticoats with a gown and fitted bodice in blood-red, and wore it under a short black riding cloak lined with taffeta.

Her flame-red hair was drawn back and secured with a silver comb - a touch she could never have afforded, nor really desired. But it played well, she felt. The actors she was about to meet would have bold personalities and swinging egos. Best to make an entrance.

She had hovered awhile over Anne's dish of rouge, never having worn make-up before, then brushed a little onto each cheek.

It felt perfectly theatrical.

The Strand was shrouded in gloom at the early hour, and the myriad windows in the towering townhouses were dark. Aside from their echoing footsteps, the only other sound was a man snoring in a doorway. A fine drizzle was falling, and a crescent moon hovered overhead, all but obscured behind charcoal-black clouds.

Following Drury Lane, now stilled, they passed the alleyway leading to the rear of the King's Playhouse and, as before, turned left onto Russell Street.

At the top of Bridges Street, Pepys stopped. "The entrance to the theatre lies that way, Abigail. Do you wish to see it?"

When she declined, he persisted. "Yet you have not visited the place, as I am aware? How do you propose to play the part of an experienced actress?"

She tapped her nose. "Fear not, sir. I've a tale prepared for the King's illustrious company."

"As you wish," said Pepys, bidding them continue.

Crossing over Bow Street, Russell Street opened out into a stunning public square bounded by railings, of such size that it stopped them in their tracks.

"Covent Garden piazza," said Pepys. "Have you visited before?"

Abby shook her head, taking it all in. "Mary told me of it - she buys fresh produce here for your larder - but I've never had cause to visit. I wish now I had."

Jacob said nothing. This was his first sight of the piazza as well, though he would not admit it. Places frequented by large crowds tended to set his teeth on edge.

"Designed by the estimable Inigo Jones," Pepys said, "and commissioned by the fourth Earl of Bedford. The same gentleman whose family own the land upon which the King's Playhouse was built." Drawing a breath, he muttered to himself, "But that I had half their wealth." Then he added brightly, "Mr Jones, I seem to recall, took his inspiration from the great squares of Paris and Italy."

The piazza was bordered on either side by stuccoed and pilastered townhouses, four and five storeys high, as elegant as they were tall.

Ahead, across the square, stood a dazzling building with a grand portico, supported by four limestone columns, Roman in style. It appeared untainted by London's smoke and soot, as if protected by some divine power.

"St Paul's Church," said Pepys, noting his inquisitors' gaze. "Is it not magnificent? Built when this square was first laid out, some thirty years ago."

Signs of life were stirring, and the overhead dusk was beginning to pale.

A porter passed by carrying a yoke of baskets across his shoulders, brimming with cabbages. Here and there, stalls were being erected of canvas with wooden frames, bringing to mind the booths of Temple Street at the Frost Fair.

Elsewhere, hand-carts were being unloaded of their produce for the popular fruit and vegetable market. A donkey, tied to a post, was urinating noisily.

"Shall we?" said Pepys.

Browne's Coffee House nestled behind the church, one of several narrow establishments tucked into the arched arcade that stretched west beyond the piazza. A sign outside marked its presence, and the door stood partly ajar, releasing a faint breath of smoke and roasting coffee beans, and the words of men arguing.

"I shall not play it!"

"And London shall not mourn!"

Jacob stooped to whisper into Abby's ear. "The first was Hugh Faybourne, the comic. The other, Dorian Lucius."

She nodded, smiling.

She seems so perfectly poised, he thought, feeling a surge of pride. *If only I had her composure.*

Within, the room was dark-wooded and dingy, lit by a smattering of wall sconces and the flames from a hearth. Low beams crossed the ceiling, and theatrical notices were pinned haphazardly about the walls, several browned and curling at the edges.

A sleepy-eyed server was tending a coffee pot warming by the fire, and bottles lined on a shelf behind his counter confirmed that stronger drink was also sold here – brandy, wine, gin – for those with frayed nerves or theatrical hours to keep.

In the centre of the room was a long rectangular table, around which glowering men were seated, all eyes intent upon the arriving party.

Pepys and Jacob recognised them - bar one - at once. Faybourne, Lucius, Marwood and Tresillion, each dressed soberly in street garb, though Jacob noticed Faybourne was wearing a long, hooked false nose.

The fifth man was young, not much older than Abby, who had turned twenty during the Frost Fair. He wore no periwig, though his tousled blond hair almost resembled one. His bright eyes darted about, his ears pricked, alert for every whisper.

He wore a dishevelled dark velvet coat and his ink-stained fingers, drumming restlessly on a pile of papers before him, were so long and bony they might almost have belonged to a witch.

Thomas Tresillion rose as Pepys and his inquisitors joined the table, his face a mask of barely guarded disdain. Peregrine Marwood raised an elegant eyebrow.

"This is your actress, Pepys?" Tresillion said. "Abigail Harcourt? I confess, she is striking. Thus I should remember her, had I ere set eyes on the lady." Lowering his tone, he added, "Yet I have not."

Even the server turned to stare.

And the fire crackled.

Abby stepped forward, swishing her petticoats before her. "And which of you illustrious rogues is to play my Othello?"

Tickling Marwood under the chin, she whispered softly, "Will it be you, Peregrine Marwood, doyen of all London, who commands the stage like the King's general?"

Clasping her wrist, he slowly removed her hand, sullen and intent.

Unruffled, she moved on to Lucius, bending to dust his cheek with puckered lips. "Or you, Mr Dorian Lucius, who sends the ladies' hearts aflutter." She smiled coyly. "And I can well see why, you naughty fellow."

Lucius grinned salaciously, a vision of self-satisfaction. Distractedly, he loosened his cravat.

"Or you, Hugh Faybourne," she purred, turning to the comic, who was already pushing himself back in his chair, but could not escape her. "Will it be you?"

Jacob nudged Pepys, eager for the quip.

Yet when Faybourne opened and closed his mouth, no sound emerged. The poor fellow looked terrified.

Before he could react, Abby whipped off his false nose and tossed it to the server. "It seems not!" she declared, stepping back and bowing.

Lucius was on his feet, applauding wildly. "Bravo, madam!"

Even Marwood could not conceal his delight, shoulders juddering with suppressed laughter.

Faybourne scrambled upright, sending his chair clattering backwards, and stormed to the door, shooting Abby a filthy look as he passed.

Jacob called after him, "I do apologise for my colleague's behaviour, sir. I found your false nose delightfully witty."

The comic stopped, swivelled, and stared. "'Twas not worn for comic purposes, you clodpot! I wear it to avoid being recognised."

With that, he was gone, leaving uproarious mirth in his wake.

Tresillion held out a chair for Abby, who sat with the delicacy of a queen.

"Consider yourself hired," he told her.

Chapter Sixteen

A New Work

No audition was required, such had been Abby's bravura performance. Lucius could not take his eyes off her, and Jacob found himself warily simmering, then questioning his motives.

It was plain to all that Abby could look after herself. Then why his concern that a gentleman might try to take advantage?

Pepys, for his part, had been spellbound. Having considered himself familiar with her potential, he now realised he had barely grazed the surface. What, he wondered with pride, have I unleashed?

Barely four months ago, that girl - *young woman* - had been responsible for scouring his chamberpots and boiling his laundry. Naturally, he had shown her undue kindness and allowed her a freer rein than most gentlemen of his standing might. He had no children; it had pleased him.

Yet, as his inquisitor, her ingenuity, her composure, and her sheer audacity had surpassed even his most improbable expectations.

He, too, was finding it hard to tear his gaze from her.

The stranger in their midst introduced himself as Jack Sawyer, author of plays.

"Which plays, sir?" Pepys asked.

Before Sawyer could reply, Tresillion tapped repeatedly on the table, attracting Pepys's attention.

"Must I remind you, Pepys, that you play no part in the King's Company?" Tresillion said. "I am grateful to you for introducing me to Mistress Harcourt, who has just claimed my stage as if it were already hers. But I must bid you farewell, sir."

Nodding sheepishly to Jacob, the pair of them rose.

"Are my words clear enough for you?" Tresillion added.

Pepys did not dignify him with a reply.

"To business," the manager said, once the coffee-house door had closed.

Sawyer, Abby learned, had been raised among a travelling theatre troupe, performing in market halls and inn yards from Norfolk to Kent. Having grown into roles in their drolls, songs and farces, he had become captivated by the power words held over an audience, and later turned his hand to writing.

It was during a performance of his first full-length play - The Masque of Sighs, staged in Norwich - that a member of the Duke's Company happened to be in attendance.

Impressed, he had brought him to London.

"...And to the Duke's Company, I assume?" Abby asked, all too aware of the connection to her nemesis, Edmund Fletcher.

Everyone stared.

Tresillion, coffee bowl halfway to his lips, held it there.

Careless, Abby realised. She had overstepped the mark. This version of Abigail Harcourt was an actress, not inquisitor, and she would do well to remember it.

She giggled, brushing at her bodice. "Have I spilled something?"

Tresillion lowered his bowl, while Lucius's eyeballs bulged.

"You'll have to forgive me, gentlemen," she added quickly. "I'm a glutton for curiosity."

It would buy her some leeway, she hoped.

Sawyer smiled nervously. "Aye, em, m-mistress, 'twas indeed the Duke's Company to which I was... to which I was...em..." He spoke as if walking on hot coals.

Tresillion put him out of his misery. "Mr Sawyer's play, this Masque of Sighs here," he motioned to the stack of papers, "was indeed bound for Fletcher's stage. Until I took it from him."

Sawyer dropped his head, hoping it might render him invisible.

Tresillion prodded him. "I offered him more money, did I not?"

Sawyer only squirmed.

"And when shall I see some of this coin, Tresillion?" Marwood cut in. "I grow impatient of your excuses."

Lucius, beside him, nodded.

The manager pushed himself upright. "When shall I see some of this coin, *Mr* Tresillion?"

As Marwood leaned across the table, Abby spotted a patch of white ceruse he had failed to wash off, nestling in the corner of his eye.

"Your company would perish, were I to follow Lansmere to the Duke's." The actor spat out the words.

Yet Tresillion only broke into peals of laughter. When finally he stopped, he jabbed a finger in Abby's direction. "See how readily I replace a principal player?"

With a snarl, Marwood stormed off in Faybourne's wake.

"Fear not, my dear," Lucius told Abby, his hand lingering on her knee. "He does that all the time. An actor's temperament."

"Aye." Tresillion snorted. "He'll be back."

Abby glanced at Sawyer, who looked utterly petrified.

"What, then, will be my role?" Abby asked.

"Whatever it is, I'm sure you shall make it your own," Lucius said, his tone dripping butter. "Already I am on tenterhooks to play our first scene together."

Tresillion sighed wearily. "Do be quiet, Lucius. Subtlety is not your forté." He turned to Abby. "He was the same with Franny - and look what became of her."

"We'll perform Mr Sawyer's Masque of Sighs?" Abby asked, pointedly avoiding Lucius's misted gaze. "I'm told you were performing The Maid's Tragedy when Mistress Jenkins met her tragic end. Could I not reprise her part, since the company are familiar with the work?"

She noticed Sawyer nodding enthusiastically.

But it was not to be.

"I did consider it," Tresillion said, "and cast the idea aside. Franny was adored, and 'twould be folly to attempt to replace her. The audience would be up in arms - a mutiny - and your time in the King's Company short-lived."

"I understand, sir. I'm happy to play any role you assign me." She heard her voice waver, but smiled. "I'm eager to begin."

Apparently satisfied, Tresillion turned to Sawyer. "Mr Sawyer? What is her role?"

The Masque of Sighs' author finally cracked a smile. "You, em, Mistress Harcourt, are Queen Seraphina, a conflicted m-monarch haunted by… by visions. On the eve of her, um, betrothal." He looked to Tresillion, who motioned for him to continue. "Three, um, Spirits guide her through a realm… through a realm of shadows. Their names are, um, Power, um, Love and F-Folly. Each scene lays bare a different… a different, um, sin. In Act III alone…"

"Aye, Mr Sawyer, I thank you, but I need not the entire plot," Tresillion cut in, adding in a mutter, "Not at that pace."

"A-as you wish, sir."

"Don't stand on ceremony, Sawyer. Call me Mr Tresillion." The manager rose. "To the theatre, I think. We open in two days, and there is a great deal of work to be done."

Chapter Seventeen

Rehearsal

Abby followed Tresillion and Lucius through the rear door to the theatre, emerging into the passageway that led to the manager's office. She knew Pepys and Jacob had entered by the same door the day before, and knew also that Tibbet had surprised them there with the annotated cue roll. Jacob had been thorough in his briefing. She was counting on it.

The tiniest detail, she had learned, might be key to unmasking a murderer - or allowing them their freedom.

When Tresillion ushered her into the tiring-house, she had to quell a gasp. The place was alive. A boy ran past with a pot of glue; somebody else shouted for thread. In one corner, an older man was darning a pair of stockings, while another called up to a fellow among the rafters.

Players paced back and forth, rolls of paper in hand, learning their parts. Nobody paid Abby's group the slightest notice, so absorbed were they in their own roles.

Beyond the timber wall ahead, where she assumed was the stage, came the thuds and crashes of scenery being dragged down and heaved about.

Voices hollered, hammers struck, lines were recited.

The whole place smelled of dust, wax and devotion.

Devotion to the joy of theatre.

Abby found herself instantly sold.

When Tresillion excused himself – his office beckoned, he said, promising to rejoin them imminently – Lucius linked his arm through Abby's, leaving Sawyer standing. She ached to pull away, but reminded herself she had a part to play – *a role within a role,* it occurred to her – and smiled up at her… undeniably chiselled chaperone.

"There," he said, gesturing to the three adjacent rooms against the far wall, "are the tiring-rooms of the principal actors. Marwood, myself, and Faybourne. Mine is central, which befits my role in the company, do you not think?"

He waited for her to agree, before pointing out the two larger rooms the other side of the tiring-house door. "Nearest us," he squeezed her arm, "is the tiring-room of the walk-ons, and beyond that, Tresillion's office."

"Where did Franny retire to?"

"Ah! That would be here."

To their right was a boarded wooden room, smaller than the others, bearing a door and no window.

"'Twas once Tibbet's workshop," he said. "Franny demanded its use, having deemed herself above undressing among the walk-ons."

"Then where does Tibbet work?"

"Over there." Lucius pointed out another room, across the tiring-house. "He built it for himself, after Franny ousted him."

That, too, had no window. Abby noticed a padlock on the door.

And there before it, a bare table, with clutter piled to one side - among it, a pair of silver goblets.

The props table, she thought, imagining Franny Jenkins's corpse, cold and prostrate upon it.

The inquisitor was saved from a tour of Lucius's tiring-room by the timely return of the theatre manager.

Calling for his acting company to assemble, Tresillion led them through a curtained doorway, via a wing, onto the stage itself. A few gruff orders later, hoardings were dragged clear of the apron, and the carpenters and painters banished to the rear.

"Hammer quietly!" he ordered.

Abby heard none of it. She was gazing out into the house, lost in admiration.

From the apron at the front of the stage, she felt as if she were standing at the prow of a ship, seeing not an ocean stretching ahead, but people. Row upon row of them, stretching back and climbing into darkness. A blur of faces, fans and feathers. Expectation. Exhilaration. *Adoration.*

Never had she felt so small – and yet, standing there in the King's Playhouse, so important.

This vast arena, she realised, was a temple to illusion, and all those people out there…

"Abigail! Abigail Harcourt!"

They're calling my name, she thought.

The hand on her shoulder made her start so acutely that the comb in her hair became dislodged. Flustered, she pushed it back into place.

Turning, she saw Thomas Tresillion smiling.

He draped an arm around her shoulder. She noticed how short he was, for such a powerful man.

"I built all this myself," he said, sweeping an arm from the boxes to the galleries. "At a cost of one thousand five hundred pounds. Magnificent, is it not?"

Abby declined to point out that she could not have afforded even the cheapest seats.

"I'm in awe, sir," she said.

"Good," said Tresillion. "Shall we begin?"

Marwood and Faybourne, as expected, had slunk back to the theatre after their tantrums in the coffee house. Lucius was there, too, forming part of a loose semi-circle of actors, each clutching their cue rolls.

They made an odd company; predominantly men, but varied in age, appearance and bearing. One woman, high-cheeked with braided golden hair, seemed to be staring at her. When Abby cast her a questioning glance, she turned away.

Abby noticed a finely honed young buck, barely older than herself, standing beside Lucius. His long hair was the colour of midnight, and his expression hovered somewhere between conviction and angst.

He seems a man I can do business with, she thought.

She sidled in between him and Lucius. "Abigail Harcourt," she said.

"Philip Tredwell," came the dulcet reply, though he eyed her guardedly. "You're the new actress."

"For my sins."

"What parts have you played?"

It caught Abby off-guard. The first challenge to her credentials, and from one of the younger players, no less. She forced a smile, but the gesture was not returned.

She would have to earn her place.

Thinking fast, she replied, "I've played in cellars 'neath inns and taverns, in abandoned chapels and stinking rooms above coffee houses. I've played Calantha in The Broken Heart and Lady Would-Be in Volpone. I've been a serving maid, a milkmaid, a mute attendant and a hopeless wretch in the stocks. Fear not, Mr Tredwell - I've played my parts."

Slowly, Tredwell's lips curled into a smile. "You may call me Pip," he said.

"And you may call me Abby."

"Consider it done," interjected a new voice - Lucius's. "*Abby Harcourt,*" he oozed with a bow.

With an appalled look, Pip stepped between he and Abby.

Lucius laughed. "Dearest Pip, this lady needs no protection from I! My intentions are ever those of a perfect gentleman."

Abby reached for Pip's wrist and gave it a gentle squeeze. The young man shook his head.

When Tresillion arrived, Sawyer cowering at his rear, Peregrine Marwood strode forward, slapping his cue roll into his palm.

"Lucius's part outweighs mine," he said, then jabbed a finger toward Faybourne. "Even the comic's roll is fatter. Yet I'm the one who fills this house. The one they hail as the King's Company's finest. Explain yourself, sir. As a shareholder, I expect to be afforded a choice of roles."

There's one shareholder, thought Abby. She just had to weed out the others.

It took a while for the actor to be placated. Time was too short for the usual consultation, Tresillion explained. Marwood was to play the Spirit of Power, among most magisterial of all, second only to Fate himself – who made no appearance, but was evoked by a roll of thunder.

Tresillion sighed. "Unless you'd prefer that role?"

Lucius was to play the Spirit of Love, and Faybourne the Spirit of Folly. Both had a few more lines, but only because Power required no verbosity, the manager explained. His presence alone was command enough. He was omnipotent.

"Does that suit you, Mr Marwood?" Tresillion said, in a tone suggested it had better.

Chastened, Marwood returned to his place in the semi-circle, accompanied by rising mutters and Lucius's broad smirk.

"Silence!" Tresillion barked, and ushered Abby forward. "Mistress Harcourt here – given Mistress Jenkins's tragic absence – is to play the Queen, Seraphina. She stands at the heart of the masque, torn 'twixt three forces. In the end, she ascends to face judgement, and in doing so, lays bare the truth of them all."

Marwood opened his mouth to speak.

"Nay, Mr Marwood," Tresillion cut him off. "She has fewer lines than you."

With that, the rehearsal began. Each actor read their part aloud for the first time, familiarising themselves with lines and cues. Tresillion sat with the writer, Sawyer, in the front row of the pit, cringing occasionally, and making notes with a quill. Every now and then, he would take a surreptitious swig from a silver hip flask.

For Abby, it all passed in a daze. One moment, she was speaking her opening line, her voice echoing thinly into the empty house, sounding smaller and more timid than she had ever heard it.

"You wear strange faces, yet I know your voices from my dreams. Why do you taunt me so?"

The next, she was nearing the play's climax, when Seraphina faced her final judgement at Fate's hand. Her heart pounded in her ears, and more than once she missed her cue. But then, so had everyone else - even Marwood, she noted with wry satisfaction - and both Lucius and Pip, on either side, had offered encouraging words.

As the play progressed, her confidence grew, until she and Seraphina seemed as one. Acting, she realised, was no different from her role as inquisitor. In both, she stepped into the guise of somebody she was not. Somebody of standing, who commanded attention, to whom others must defer. It struck a chord.

Perhaps I'm equal to this? she wondered.

"If I must be drawn to Heaven," she enunciated, cue roll held out before her, "then let it be on the wings of truth, not in treachery's embrace..." She stopped, peering out into the auditorium. "Mr Tresillion, you mean to have me lifted in the air?"

A chorus of groans rang out.

"This… girl is no actress!" Marwood declared. "Let me play the part!"

Tresillion rose imperiously. "*Mr* Marwood. You cannot play the Queen, since the Spirit of Power and she share several scenes. And, must I remind you, since the King himself decreed that women's roles be played by women."

"His edict is a nonsense! It makes a mockery of my stage."

"*My* stage, Peregrine. Not yours. I am His Majesty's patentee, not you." Tresillion pushed up his ruffled sleeves. "In my view, Mistress Harcourt has conducted herself most admirably, and makes a fine queen in Mr Sawyer's new piece. I propose we complete our remaining lines and then break for supper, after which we shall play it again. And again."

He had to shout over the resulting rumble of discontent. "For we open in two days' time, and, I am reliably informed," Tresillion paused, "that His Majesty himself will be in attendance."

While the company celebrated - a full house guaranteed, once word spread - Abby sighed inwardly. It was the last thing she needed: the added weight of the King's presence.

And that man was as incorrigible as Lucius.

Chapter Eighteen

The Cock

The company retired to The Cock tavern on Bow Street, barely a stroll away in the direction of the piazza. Abby was eager to visit the establishment, which Pepys had mentioned more than once in aghast tones.

He would recount - with barely concealed glee - how he had learned from Sir William Batten of the trial of Sir Charles Sedley, wit and dramatist.

In June of 1663, Sedley, accompanied by Lord Buckhurst (Charles Sackville) and Sir Thomas Ogle, had become riotously drunk in The Cock, run by one Oxford Kate. (Abby was especially keen to glimpse Kate, who, by all accounts, presided like an errant monarch over a tavern frequented by rakes, thieves, fops - and members of the theatrical set.)

Sedley, Buckhurst and Ogle belonged to the notorious drinking club known as the Ballers, whose cardinal rule was that no man should speak of another's indiscretions following a night of inebriation.

That afternoon in The Cock, few along Bow Street could have missed their antics.

Sedley had hired a private room above the tavern, where the trio washed down platters of meat with a jug of wine, or five. True to form, they stripped naked, flung open the windows, and paraded themselves on the balcony before a burgeoning crowd.

At this point in the tale, Pepys would grow coy, saying what followed was not fit for a lady's ears. He would, however, recall Sedley preaching to the onlookers in profane and blasphemous language, then performing an act of treason so lewd that outraged citizens pelted him with stones and rotten fruit. .

At trial, the Lord Chief Justice, Robert Foster, told Sedley it was because of him "that God's judgement and anger hang over us", and fined him five hundred pounds. Abby calculated that, during her years as Pepys's servant, it would have taken her two centuries to pay off such a sum.

Sedley – also Member of Parliament for New Romney in Kent – merely petitioned Charles II for leniency, and the King, who saw plenty of himself in the rake, declined to collect the money.

As Tresillion opened the door to The Cock, a grey cloud of smoke escaped, thick with hollers and cackles. Abby, bringing up the rear, hunched her shoulders and stepped inside.

She was met by a man crawling on all fours, grunting like a pig, who began snuffling around her ankles. His veined cheeks resembled a map, and his teeth were largely absent. When she nudged him aside with her foot, a cheer went up.

At the far end of the tavern, near a rickety stair that led to the private rooms and guest chambers above, another man lay slumped across a virginal, dead to the world. Behind him, two companions pranced and tittered, holding a candle to his periwig in a bid to set it alight. Nobody moved to stop them.

The place reeked, of so many competing odours that Abby cared not to discern any particular one.

When the King's Company claimed three different tables, she made sure to secure a seat next to Pip. The young man seemed affable enough, and, she hoped, would not grow suspicious of her questions.

"Thomas Tresillion!" came the brittle cry. "As I live and breathe!"

Oxford Kate, thought Abby, craning her neck to see.

"Not for long, eh, lads?" came the drawled riposte of a nearby drunk, whom Kate cheerfully cuffed with the back of her hand.

Tresillion, seated by the hearth with Marwood, Lucius and Faybourne, stood and embraced her.

"How long has it been?" she asked.

Tresillion counted on his pale, bony fingers. "Ten hours."

They slapped each other's backs.

As they did, Kate spotted Abby, shoved Tresillion away, and headed for her table.

"You the new Franny?" she asked.

Word travels fast, Abby thought. "I could never fill her shoes."

"Why not find out?" came Kate's reply. "She kept a room upstairs. Her things are untouched."

Abby studied her, unsure whether she was jesting.

Oxford Kate was smaller than she had imagined – scarcely broader than Abby herself – but the thin lines around her pursed lips and the resolve in her bloodshot gaze made clear she was not to be trifled with. She wore a russet smock and cream apron, her hair tousled as if she had recently wrestled.

Her skin seemed leathery – or perhaps browned by the miasma of the tavern's decay.

Abby liked her at once. "You and Franny were friends?"

Kate smirked. "What's one death among hundreds, duck?"

As she turned to go, Abby grabbed her skirt. When Kate scowled down, she hastily withdrew her hand.

"I-I meant to ask…" Abby heard herself stammer, and realised she felt more cowed by this slight tavern keeper than by any towering lord. She had seen behind the facades of powerful men as they dropped their guard in Pepys's company. This woman took no prisoners.

Swallowing, she added, "Who do you think murdered her?"

Kate huffed. "I'm not paid to think."

And with that, she turned on her heel.

Pip nudged Abby. "Why does Franny's death interest you?"

"So I'm prepared if they come for me next." She laughed unconvincingly.

Pip bit his lower lip, and nodded.

"Tell me about flying," Abby added quickly. "How shall I ascend to the heavens?"

Having explained the pulleys and ropes that would hoist the fledgling actress into the rafters, supping beer all the while, Pip's words began to slur. Abby, who had drunk a similar, modest amount, was relieved to feel sober, and hoped the drink might loosen her companion's tongue.

The young actor's supper comprised a single boiled egg, which Abby paid for. Pip was penniless, he claimed, but promised soon to pay her back.

When a platter laden with a plump boiled lobster and pickles was set before Thomas Tresillion, to the evident consternation of his assembled company, Abby seized her chance.

"Who owns shares in the King's Company?" she asked Pip, grinning as if they were exchanging riddles.

Pip snorted. "Not I, that's for sure."

"Aye, but whom? Marwood admitted as much. I assume Lucius, too? And Faybourne?"

"Why would I be privy to such secrets? Marwood's boastful, at times loose-lipped. The others are more guarded." He shifted in his seat. "Why so many questions? They make my head ache."

All at her table glanced up from their food, and Abby was relieved to see Tresillion still intent on his. *Stay your hand*, she told herself, vexed by her own haste. *'Tis early days.*

"How did you become an actor?" she asked.

Pip beamed, his flawless features catching the candle-light. His neighbour, a rotund, grizzled old man with but a single line in The Masque of Sighs, tutted and returned to his oysters.

"My mother was a seamstress, and my father a carpenter. She sewed stage clothes, he built scenery. They worked all their lives in playhouses, and I grew up among them. 'Twas my father's dying wish that I become a principal actor in the King's Company."

The old man snorted. "Some way off that."

His neighbour chimed in, "Helps that he butters up Lucius, hangs on his every word." Then he launched into a nasal impersonation of Pip: "'Aye, Mr Lucius. Nay, Mr Lucius. Three bags full, Mr Lucius.'"

"Reckon 'e's in love!" the old man chided.

And the two of them bumped elbows, giggling like children.

Pip glared. "Dorian Lucius is a master of his trade. Perhaps the greatest actor in all London. I do well to learn at his side."

"Oh aye," the old man said. "And you're its finest walk-on."

The situation was slipping from Abby's grasp.

"When did you join the King's Company?" she asked Pip.

He turned to her and narrowed his eyes. "More questions?"

"'An innocent one, I assure you."

Pip took another bite of the egg. "I was among the first, after the bleak years of the Interregnum. It felt like life returning. I..."

The old man butted in again. "Fell out wi' Mr Marwood, didn't yer, lad? I remember it clear. Jonson's Alchemist. I was playing…"

"*I did not fall out with Mr Marwood,*" Pip snapped. "I…"

"Aye yer did. Marwood wanted the role o' Dol Common – besides the lead, mind – but Tresillion told 'im he was too old to play 'er. Give you the part instead. That didn't sit well, did it?"

In a trice, Pip was out of his seat. "Be silent, you grotty old man!"

As the old man stood, looming over Pip, a hush fell.

A slow hand-clap started, accompanied by a chant.

"Fight! Fight! Fight!"

"I'll have no fighting in my house!" Kate bellowed.

"That's a lie, for starters!" came the heckle, followed by a hail of supper's remnants.

Stepping outside, Abby felt a hand on her shoulder. She turned to find Oxford Kate, a skewed version of motherly concern on her face.

"You asked me who murdered Franny. I wouldn't trust me if I told you," she said, then, drawing Abby closer, added, "And I wouldn't trust none o' them, neither."

Glancing up Bow Street, Abby assured herself the rest of the company were too far off to overhear. "You know of Edmund Fletcher?"

Kate arched a brow. "I wouldn't put it past him."

"Wouldn't put what past him?"

"Murdering poor Franny!" Kate laughed.

Abby thought twice about hushing her. "Have you seen him of late?"

"Not since they fell out."

Abby frowned. "Fell out?"

"With Tresillion. Over Lansmere. Don't you know? Since he defected to the Duke's and took the play with him."

"I…"

"Abigail!" came Tresillion's call. He had stopped, his actors too, beckoning with exaggerated impatience.

"I have to go," she said.

Chapter Nineteen

Bad Penny

Returning to the theatre, Abby was uncomfortably aware she had learned precious little. Still, she consoled herself that she had made a connection - perhaps even gained an ally - in Pip Tredwell. Time, she reasoned, was on her side.

Unless the murderer strikes again.

She pushed the thought away and found herself yawning. The long, sleepless night was catching up with her. So swift had been her plunge into theatrical life that she had scarcely had a moment to breathe, let alone take stock.

Then she tripped.

She was in the alleyway off Drury Lane, leading to the tiring-house door, barely wide enough for two abreast. Down she went, onto the frigid, filthy stone, grit scraping into her palms. She assumed she had been distracted, careless - until she looked up.

A woman loomed over her, sinewy and sneering.

It was the same blonde actress who had stared at her on the stage.

"You alright there, my blossom?" she said. "Took a nasty tumble, didn't yer?"

She held out a hand, then pulled it away when Abby reached for it.

"Wouldn't want yer to take a nastier fall, would we now?"

And she was gone.

Abby felt hands around her waist, helping her to her feet.

"Are you hurt?" It was Pip Tredwell.

"Aye," she replied uncertainly, studying her scratched hands. "Who is that?"

"Clara Lovick. She expected to take Franny's role. Until…"

"I came along."

Pip sighed. "You should watch her."

"Fear not, I shall." Abby brushed down her gown. "Thank you kindly."

If her fall had been a shock, worse was yet to come.

Entering the tiring-house, a raised voice rang out. She recognised it at once, and her pulse quickened.

Will.

What in God's name was her brother doing here?

If he saw her, he might give her away. One careless word, and they would know she was no actress, but a spy in their midst.

And there he was, holding court to a gaggle of actors and attendants outside Matt Tibbet's workshop. A stack of papers sat beside him on the props table. Broadsides, fresh from his press?

She recalled Will mentioning a Mr Eversleigh and a commission that would keep him working into the night. Was Eversleigh somehow tied to the theatre?

Should I hide?

She stood frozen, painfully aware of her garish attire, knowing that any sudden movement might draw his attention. If he saw her, he would surely call out, and she would be done.

"Abby!"

It jolted her into action.

As fast as her legs would carry her – without quite breaking into a trot and arousing suspicion – she made for her brother. He was waving cheerily now, turning his audience's attention on her.

Abby fixed a grin. "William! What brings you here? Such a pleasant surprise."

She could feel the eyes on her. They burned. Still she pressed on, her dainty feet, mercifully hidden beneath her petticoats, pumping like a blacksmith's hammer.

"William!" she gasped, arriving breathless before him.

Faybourne was among the onlookers, and that dreadful Lovick woman, still staring.

"How goes it?" Will asked. "This is my…"

"I'm his sister," she cut in swiftly. "William here is the most loyal brother a girl could ask for. He's seen my every performance. Haven't you, William?"

She saw confusion cloud his face, but thankfully all were watching her.

"I-I thought you…," he faltered. "Mr Pepys…?"

"Whose kind recommendation secured my part, among all these marvellous actors!" Her gaze bore into him, willing him to follow her lead.

He only seemed more bewildered. "Are you…?"

"Indeed I am!" she cried, throwing up her arms and spinning with feigned joy. "I've joined the King's Company." Then quickly she added, "And what brings you here?"

Faybourne spoke up with a withering drawl. "He was about to read out Eversleigh's critique of yesterday's production. Before he was so rudely interrupted." He wafted a hand. "Pray, continue, would you?"

With a sideways glance at his sister, Will obeyed.

"A True and Accurate Account of Diverse Misadventures in the Theatre Royal, with Particular Reflection on Tragedies Most Unnatural."

Groans rippled through the small crowd just as Marwood arrived, barging to the front, with Lucius bounding after him.

"What have I missed?" Lucius asked, interlocking his gloved fingers with a flourish.

"Eversleigh's up to his customary nonsense," Faybourne replied.

Lucius prodded him. "I'd have thought customary nonsense was your field?"

"Just get on with it," Faybourne snapped at Will.

"'Twas ever the nature of the King's Company to muddle tragedy with farce, but ne'er more so than yesterday, when one poor actress took it upon herself to perish in earnest."

Allowing the muttered disgust to settle, Will continued.

"Mr Beaumont & Mr Fletcher's Maid's Tragedy was presented with its usual melancholy, and its usual failure to distinguish pathos from pomposity. Peregrine Marwood, playing Melantius, commanded the stage with all the nobility and weight of a plum…"

Marwood let out a mighty, actorly roar, as Lucius buried his face in his sleeve, chortling deliriously.

"…while Dorian Lucius, the tortured Amintor, appeared to be in a different play altogether, his lustful gaze ever drawn to the well-favoured Franny Jenkins, who must surely be thankful she departed this mortal coil, save endure his puckered advances."

"How dare the scoundrel!" Lucius thundered, instantly roused to indignation. "I shall reap his pluck from guts the next time he shows his face here, and wrap them about his scrawny neck!"

Abby caught Will's gaze and saw the glint of mischief there. Clearing his throat, he pressed on, voice rising above the commotion:

"The only player to emerge from this sordid little production with his dignity intact was Hugh Faybourne, who shines with wit and gusto wherever he treads. There can be no mightier comic performer in all England. And I doubt there ever…"

Will never finished. Lucius snatched the broadside from his grasp and shredded it into tiny pieces, scattering them like bitter tears.

Faybourne watched on, chuckling quietly to himself. His purse was lighter, true - but it had been worth it to see their faces.

Chapter Twenty

The Dare

The King's Company descended into chaos, drawing Tresillion from his office to try to restore order.

With their next rehearsal delayed, Abby dragged her brother around the side of Tibbet's workshop, out of sight.

"What's going on?" Will asked quietly.

"'Tis too long a tale," she said. "All you need know is I'm here as actress, not inquisitor."

Will stifled a snort. "Actress? You?"

She sniffed. "Turns out, I'm quite adept."

"You're no longer Mr Pepys's inquisitor?"

"Hush!" She pressed a hand over his mouth, glancing about. "I'm still his inquisitor, merely playing an actress. To seek clues. They cannot know."

Clasping her wrist rather too tightly, he lowered her hand. "What's it worth?"

The Devil was in his eyes.

She stepped back. "Will?"

He shrugged. "What's it worth?"

Shaking her head with dismay, she decided to play along. "What do you want?"

"You know very well what I want, sis. To be an inquisitor, like you. Why should you have all the glory while I'm mired in Father's drudge?"

She longed to slap his pouting face, but stayed her hand. It had been years, fortunately, since she had seen this side of her brother, but he had it in him. He was stubborn as an ink stain, and not one to be dared lightly.

Once, when he was nine and she was ten, a neighbourhood boy had challenged him to leap from their roof into a rain barrel below. It was half full, and slick with algae. Still he had not hesitated, despite risking limb and possibly life.

He had landed on the rim, shattering the barrel, and returned home grazed, bruised and soaking. Their father beat him soundly for it, yet Will's expression remained defiant. Proud, even.

No, he was not one to be dared lightly.

"I can speak with Mr Pepys," Abby told him.

He beamed. "You can? And you'll recommend me?"

She nodded, unable to lie aloud.

"In place of that addle-plot, Jacob?" he persisted.

Another nod.

"Say it."

She studied him.

"*Say it.*"

What have you come to, William? she wondered, and sighed. "I'll recommend you to Mr Pepys."

"In place of that addle-plot, Jacob."

"I will not…"

"Say it, Abigail." A crooked grin. "Or I reveal your deception."

"In place of Jacob."

She stormed off, churning inside.

Will slipped through the curtain that led to the wing, then down to the passageway that would take him out of the King' Playhouse, smiling all the way.

Chapter Twenty-One

Christopher Beeston

*E*dmund Fletcher never did finish his performance of *The Martyr of Elmleigh* at the midsummer feast. Once he had gathered his senses, his father, Giles, dragged him by the ear through the estate gates, and ordered him never again to darken his doors.

Edmund hated the man. He was boorish and overbearing.

Had it not been for the purse of gold coins his mother, Agatha, slipped into his hand that night, his future might have looked distinctly less rosy. She was a decent sort, really - if only she had stood up to Giles more, as he had.

Retrieving his little bundle of belongings from the ditch where he had slept, he made for the creek to seek out Jonas Kettley's barge. Kettley was reluctant to allow him aboard, having heard about the lad's antics at the feast, but Edmund was insistent.

"You're like my mother," he chided him. "He's only a man, after all."

When Giles learned of his errant son's passage to London - aboard his finest grain barge - he dismissed Kettley on the spot. The old man had served Giles's father before him, and his father before that.

Theatrical zeal ran through Edmund's veins.

He took lodgings at St-Giles-in-the-Fields, a cheap, dingy, dangerous quarter riven with rats and cutpurses, but walking distance from the Cockpit. The theatre became his church of sorts, and he drank in play after play. James Shirley's The Traitor, The Gamester, The Young Admiral; John Ford's 'Tis A Pity She's a Whore and The Broken Heart; Philip Massinger's The Roman Actor and The City Madam. Works by Middleton, Jonson, Shakespeare, Kid, Heywood, Rowley...

They made him feel alive. He memorised entire scenes, copying them out by candlelight, and befriended a few of the players, having accosted them in local taverns. As his funds dwindled, he grew ever more desperate to become involved.

The Cockpit's manager was one Christopher Beeston, a man marred by a scandalous past, who also ran the Red Bull playhouse in Clerkenwell. Beeston's company, Queen Henrietta's Men, was a popular rival to the much-vaunted King's Men of Blackfriars Theatre; he also maintained a company of child actors, known as Beeston's Boys.

One evening, Edmund took his chance. Having followed the manager to his home on Drury Lane, he accosted him in his doorway and begged for a chance to join the Boys.

Beeston looked the sallow-faced teenager up and down, unimpressed, yet somewhat taken by his gumption. "You know the part of Vindice, lad?"

"I know it well, sir," Edmund replied. He had seen The Revenger's Tragedy two days in succession at Beeston's theatre. It was one of the roles he had transcribed.

Vindice was a poetic soul, a revolutionary of sorts, seeking vengeance from a man of power and privilege. He spoke to Edmund's very bones.

"Then play the part, lad," said Beeston.

Edmund looked around. It was a summer's evening, and Drury Lane bustled with the well-to-do and those who would fleece them.

He took a step back, drew breath, and began. "Thou sallow picture of my poisoned love, my study's ornament, thou shell of death. Once the bright face of my betrothed lady..."

He stopped abruptly. Beeston's cheeks were fit to burst, as he struggled to control his mirth.

Edmund flushed. "Do I amuse you, sir?"

That encounter set his course. Never again would he act.

Instead, he vowed revenge on Christopher Beeston.

He would take on the tawdry lout at his own game. He would form his own theatrical company, build his own playhouse, and become London's greatest theatre manager.

He still had gold, a full set of wits - and he burned.

Oh, how he burned with righteousness.

Chapter Twenty-Two

Brief Encounter

Rounding Tibbet's workshop, Abby barged straight into an old woman loitering outside his door, all but bowling her over. A couple of oranges tumbled from her basket, which Abby retrieved and returned, apologising.

As she did so, a thought struck her. "Were you… eavesdropping?"

The old woman wafted a saffron fan. "Your secret's safe with me, don't you worry. I look after my girls."

A shiver travelled down the inquisitor's spine. She glanced around. The actors were filing towards the opposite wing for the second rehearsal, while the attendants and craftsmen remained preoccupied, preparing scenery and stage clothes.

Orange Bess introduced herself in conciliatory tones, but Abby remained guarded.

Bess stroked her upper arm. "You're a friend of Sammy Pepys?"

Abby nodded.

"And I gather he's employed you as his… inquisitor?"

Another curt nod.

"Like that tall gentleman I met only yesterday?"

That pricked Abby's ears. "Jacob? Jacob Standish?"

"Aye, that was his name. Oh my! You should've seen what became of him!"

"He told me. They put him on the stage."

Bess slapped her thigh, grinning at the memory. "Laugh? I near drenched my drawers. Sammy, too! He's incorrigible, that fine gentleman."

From the other side of the wall separating the tiring-house from the stage, Abby heard actors clearing their throats and tuning their voices.

"I have to go," she said. "You promise me that…"

Bess crossed herself. "As the Lord is my shepherd. If you're here to catch whoever murdered my lovely Franny, consider me a friend. I'd give anything to see that devil hang. Anything you need, duck, you just ask Orange Bess." She tapped her nose. "I'm the eyes and ears of this place."

Abby thought for a moment. "Who do you think did it?"

The fan fluttered again. "I have my suspicions, but 'tis too early for me to say. Wouldn't want to send the wrong person to the gallows, now, would I? Need to do some more digging meself."

"But you…"

"Nay, Abigail, you run along, or they'll begin without you, and we wouldn't want that." She ushered her away, as if herding stray hens. "Rum'un, that brother of yours," she called after the inquisitor's retreating form.

Having watched Abby brush through the curtain towards the stage, Orange Bess turned on her heel and made for one of the storerooms.

As she did so, Matt Tibbet emerged from his workshop, clutching a saw and licking his lips.

Chapter Twenty-Three

Standoff

That afternoon, and well into the evening, the King's Company read and reread their parts, beginning to plan their cues, exits, and marks upon the stage. The lack of windows meant the place remained in a constant twilight, despite the myriad candles, and Abby lost all sense of time.

The backdrop for the opening scene had been completed, and looked magnificent: a soaring gothic arcade bathed in silver moonlight, trailing with strands of ivy. Workers were still hammering away at a prop tomb, ingeniously painted to resemble marble.

Stage clothes were measured and donned for size, even as the actors rehearsed their lines.

It was all, Abby thought, wearing her actor's guise, most invigorating. Yet she was acutely aware that the inquisitor side of her task was suffering.

Mr Pepys had not paid her to play a queen, however comfortable she was becoming in the role.

During Act III, when courtiers were entertained by a jester – played inevitably by Faybourne, in addition to his role as the Spirit of Folly – Abby noticed Lucius slipping to the rear of the stage, where he arranged himself upon the Queen's throne. When he beckoned her over, a shiver ran through her.

"How are you finding the art of acting, Mistress Harcourt?" he asked. "I see you have been studying my technique. You cannot take your eyes off me."

She had indeed been watching him closely – as a suspect in her murder investigation.

"'Tis true, Mr Lucius. I count it a privilege to learn from so fine a master of his trade."

He gestured to the foot of his throne. "You may kneel and kiss the royal hand."

It was a moment before she realised he was jesting.

"And, pray," he added. "Call me Dorian."

She smiled demurely, disguising the frantic turning of her mind. *How best to broach the subject of the shares?* Then, in a flash, it came to her.

"How rich are you, Dorian?" she asked, pouting lazily.

He bellowed with laughter, and was hushed angrily by Faybourne, who had been interrupted mid-juggle.

"You're a feisty one," Lucius said, still chuckling. "If I…"

"I assume you're a shareholder?" she cut in, before his patter could gather pace.

He arched a tended eyebrow. "Why would you assume?"

"Since Mr Marwood freely admits to it, and you…"

"Are twice the actor he is?"

She flicked a strand of hair from her cheek. "Indeed."

He twirled his thumbs. "I could not possibly say."

His radiating smugness told Abby all she needed to know.

"And Mr Faybourne?" she asked.

"Why all this talk of money? 'Tis so dreadfully dull, I find. Let us speak instead…" he placed a theatrical finger to his lips, gazing upwards in mock contemplation. "Of love!"

Perfect, she thought. "I heard rumour of a note scribbled on your cue roll, said to be from Franny Jenkins. Did you love her?"

A voice cut in. "The halfwit is a glorified gigolo. He'd bed a goat if it pleased him."

Unnoticed, Peregrine Marwood had drifted within earshot, wrestling with an orange.

Lucius ignored his jibe. "Franny loved me with a passion…"

"You and half of Westminster," Marwood interjected. "You are - or should I say, *were* - a pair well-matched." His pale lips cracked a smile.

Lucius, riled, rose from his throned slouch. "She would have sunk Lansmere for me, just to win my heart!"

"Silence back there!" came Tresillion's cry.

But Abby had her answer. *These actors make such excellent suspects*, she thought, *with their egos and jabbering mouths.*

So Franny Jenkins had indeed scrawled that note to Lucius - as Matt Tibbet had suggested to Jacob - offering to ruin Benedict Lansmere's reputation. All to win Lucius's favour, it now seemed.

"This Mr Lansmere…?"

It was all she needed to ask. Marwood took the bait.

"Benedict Lansmere was the peacock of the Theatre Royal. He set the ladies' hearts a-flutter with a mere twist of his cheek. Dorian here was his understudy…"

Lucius slid from the throne and grabbed a fistful of Marwood's cravat. "I did no such thing, sir! 'Tis beneath me."

"You, sir," his rival snarled back, "were understudy more times than I care to remember, and raised to your present station not by merit - of which you have not a jot - but since Lansmere fled this company in the dead of night, taking with him Mr Shakespeare's Othello."

Lucius tightened his grip until the two men's noses were touching. His eyes bulged. "I'm minded to challenge you to a duel, sir."

"Um…" Abby tried to intervene but was swiftly cast aside.

"Then, pray, challenge away!" Marwood shot back. "You have the bravery of a plucked hen and the aim of a weathervane in a gale."

The standoff was broken by Pip Tredwell's timely arrival. "Mr Lucius, Mr Marwood - Mr Tresillion commands your presence for the next scene."

As the two simmering men broke off, Pip snatched Abby's hand and pulled her toward the wing.

"Don't go bandying words with that Lucius," he hissed.

"Whyever not?"

"Since…" Pip stopped and sighed. "Since I believe he's the reason Franny's dead."

Abby grabbed his wrists. "What makes you say that?"

He lowered his gaze. "She outshone him, and he hated it. Neither would she leave him be. Pestered him for love, though his eye was ever drawn elsewhere. He thought her beneath him, yet stealing his thunder."

"You've proof?"

"Only that of my own ears and eyes."

Chapter Twenty-Four

John Kirby

S t Clement Danes had long since chimed midnight when Abby let herself into Jacob's house on Strand Lane, to find him asleep beside Mr Pepys. Both were snoring, though one (Pepys) more gutturally than the other.

During the Frost Fair, she herself had snuggled in beside Jacob - purely for warmth. Not that the feeling of his broad (if fully clothed) chest, snug and gently heaving, had been at all displeasing. In truth, it had stirred a yearning in her.

She had learned to live without close male company since leaving the family home. Working for Mr Pepys as his maidservant during her later teens… Well, what choice had she? She could hardly have smuggled suitors into his household under his very nose. He would have been apoplectic, dismissed her on the spot, and rightly so. Besides, it would not have become her.

The young hawkers, porters and errand lads she encountered during her duties - their lolling tongues and coarse attempts at gallantry betrayed their grimy intentions.

There had been one…

Before her time with Pepys, she had lived with her mother's cousin, Mr Edward Yaxley, who ran a modest legal office. A mild, bookish man, he kept a well-stocked library of law, poetry and ancient histories, which she was encouraged to explore.

In return for his kindness, she helped his wife, Alice, manage the household and tend to their five children. They were lessons that would serve her well when she entered Pepys's service.

Had Edward not fallen sick, she might never have met John Kirby.

The son of a widowed apothecary who served the local gentry, John was seventeen - two years her elder - lanky, bright, and given to a stammer that vanished when he read aloud.

He delivered tinctures and powders to her ailing guardian and, in time, began lingering longer than necessary whenever Abby was present. It had not escaped her notice.

There was a gentleness to him that suited the Yaxley household. They began to talk. Of books and childhoods and the nearby Thames, with its teeming ships and secret nooks.

One day, as they walked in the orchard, he gifted her a copy of John Donne's Poems. She had not the heart to tell him there was one in Yaxley's library.

The final, third verse of Donne's The Good Morrow had haunted her ever since.

My face in thine eye, thine in mine appears,
And true plain hearts do in the faces rest.
Where can we find two better hemispheres,
Without sharp North, without declining West?
Whatever dies was not mixed equally;
If our two loves be one, or thou and I
Love so alike that none can slacken, none can die.

For whatever it was they had shared had died. Was it love? The ache in her chest when John's father moved his practice to Deptford - tantalising close, yet beyond her reach - told her it might have been.

Abby had thought of John that night she shared Jacob's bed.

She had woken in the small hours to find Jacob rolled tight in the blanket, and herself uncovered, trembling with cold. As she wrested back a trailing corner, it oc-curred to her, during those fleeting, strange remnants of wakefulness, that Jacob and John were not entirely dissimilar.

Both benevolent souls prone to compassion. Each at odds with the world in some awkward, introverted manner. Men she admired for their sensitivity.

She had wondered where fate might lead her. Whether Jacob, ungainly and unlikely a suitor as he was, might yet win her heart.

But before she could decide, she had fallen into an insistent, deep sleep.

Chapter Twenty-Five

The Jester

Abby was up and away from Strand Lane well before dawn, having slept fitfully. Nerves were creeping in. She cared not to admit it, but she was more anxious about her performance before London and the King than about her progress in the investigation.

Time felt tighter on the former, and the last thing she wanted was questions from Pepys at this early stage. Hence her moonlit flit.

It had occurred to her - a mere twitch of a thought, promptly dismissed - that she could always remain with the King's Company, should Pepys deem her no longer fit to serve as his inquisitor. How would the audience react to her, she wondered. Rarely had she known praise, or even gratitude, let alone… dare she conceive of it? Adulation?

Today, they would rehearse in stage attire, and she would learn to fly.

The haunting cry of an owl made Abby glance about as she reached St Clement Danes' churchyard. Silvery light tinged the ash trees, and a harsh breeze stirred the bare branches. Then she saw him - a lone figure stooped among the graves.

At first, she took him for a vagrant or drunkard and walked on. But something in the silhouette seemed familiar. *Is that… Hugh Faybourne?*

Crouching behind an overgrown wall, Abby watched as the man knelt, hat in hand, head bowed. She held her breath. After a moment, he rose, kissed his fingers and touched them gently to the earth, then slipped away through a gate opposite.

Only then did she move.

The grave was unmarked, a mound of frost-hardened earth. Nestled at its foot, propped against a large stone, sat a wooden toy. She picked it up. A carved jester, crudely painted in red and yellow, its smile was peeling and faded.

Abby felt the bite of the early morning air.

The high-heeled shoes she had borrowed from Jacob's sister *tip-tapped* up Drury Lane as she hurried after Faybourne, the sound reverberating along the wide, empty street. Every so often he stopped and looked back, but at distance seemed not to recognise her.

She meant to catch him, but was unused to walking in rich ladies' shoes. She remembered times in her childhood when her father's commissions had dried up and she had gone barefoot…

With a muttered curse, she swiped the things off and began padding after her quarry, the stones icy beneath her stockinged feet. "Mr Faybourne! Mr Faybourne!"

"What do you want, girl?" he demanded, having stopped and waited for her to catch up, hands on hips, face sullen.

She ran the last few yards and halted, panting. Her breath steamed in the frigid air.

"Why are you following me?" he demanded.

"I'm not, I assure you. Are we not both making for the same theatre?"

His nose, like a red button, looked oddly small for such an expansive face.

"Does that explain you spying on me in the church-yard?"

She grimaced. "Forgive me, sir, I didn't realise it was you. I'd never intrude upon another's grief."

"Pah!" He turned and strode on up Drury Lane.

"Hold, pray," she urged, hurrying after him.

He did not slow. "What do you want?"

"Only to discourse. To talk of the theatre."

He wheeled on her. "And why, tell me, would I stoop to oblige you? I've played Falstaff, Sir Amorous La Foole, Sir Politic Would-Be - the most fêted comic roles, on

London's finest stages. I've made knights weep with laughter and ladies swoon. Once, I had the King himself spit out his wine. And you? What claim have you to fame?"

Having no answer, she resorted to flattery. "And I'm in awe of your talent, Mr Faybourne. To my mind, it shines the brightest in the King's Company."

He raised an encouraging eyebrow.

"Aye, I had the pleasure of seeing your Falstaff," she lied. "So great were my guffaws, I feared I might burst my bodice."

"It seems I may have misjudged you," he purred, taking her arm in his. "Come, walk with me. 'Twill be my pleasure."

They talked a while, of Faybourne's triumphs and The Masque of Sighs, until Abby saw they were approaching the alleyway leading to the playhouse. *Act quickly*, she thought.

"What troubles me, sir," she began innocently enough, "is that you are not properly compensated for your standing within the King's Company."

He stopped at once, withdrew his entwined arm. "What know you of such matters?"

In truth, she had guessed. He seemed so bitter and easily goaded by his peers. "I was told in confidence."

"By whom? By that oaf Lucius?"

She said nothing, but allowed herself the slightest twitch.

"I knew it!" he cried.

Abby pressed on, groping blindly. "'Tis a grave slight upon your person, sir, and I understand your just grievance when the likes of Lucius, Marwood and…" She paused.

"And cursed Franny Jenkins!" he obliged, spluttering.

"And even…?" *Might there be others?*

"Aye, even damned Orange Bess!"

Abby's gasp betrayed her.

His eyes, glistening with outrage, narrowed to pinholes. "You knew not of Bess?"

"I… I…"

"Who is your source?"

She stepped back, crossed her heart. "I gave my word."

"You ask too many questions, girl," he muttered, and turned on his heel.

Chapter Twenty-Six

Chaos

The woman in charge of the orange girls - *granted a share of the King's Company's takings?* It made no sense. As far as Abby knew, such monies were reserved for managers, investors and actors, and Orange Bess was none of those.

She had little time to dwell on Faybourne's revelation.

If Abby had thought she would be among the first to arrive for the day's rehearsals, she was sadly misguided. Already, the tiring-house was a bustle of activity. Clatters and bangs rang out, as people milled to and fro, many of whom she failed to recognise.

The place reeked of practised efficiency and barely restrained panic. Tomorrow, the Kings Company would debut a new play by a fledgling writer, before a packed house that included the most powerful man in the realm.

From one of the rooms, she caught the undulating tones of Lucius, practising his lines. Tresillion strode past a moment later, waving his arms and barking orders. When she tried to greet him, he ignored her.

Faybourne was nowhere to be seen. Likely holed up in his own private tiring-room, brooding on injustices.

Pulling her cue roll from her satchel, Abby found a corner away from all the clamour of stomping boots, and began to read. Within moments, she was interrupted by Matt Tibbet thrusting a piece of paper into her hand.

By His Majesty's Company of Players, at the Theatre Royal. This day, being Thursday, January 17ᵗʰ, 1667, will be acted a Play called The Masque of Sighs, by Mr Sawyer.

Being the tragicomical Vision of a Queen, three Spirits, and the Fate that awaits us all.

On the eve of a Royal Betrothal, Her Majesty Serpahina is visited by three masked Spirits, being Love, Power, and Folly, each bearing memories from her past and promises for her future. One speaks Truth, the others only Ruin.

With celestial machines, rare music, and a flight never before dared upon the English stage.

The Spirit of Power, Mr. Marwood; The Spirit of Love, Mr. Lucius; The Spirit of Folly, Mr. Faybourne; Queen Seraphina, Mrs. Harcourt. The Play will begin at Three o'clock exactly. Boxes, 5s.; Pit, 3s.; First Gallery, 2s. 6d.; Upper Gallery, 1 s.

It was a playbill, announcing tomorrow's performance. Abby's eyes were torn in two directions: to her name, printed beneath the King's crest - an honour that seemed unimaginable - and to the phrase "a flight never before dared upon the English stage".

That, she realised with a sickly swallow, would be her.

The day began with another reading of parts on the stage, with plans to rehearse in full attire that afternoon. It could not have fared much worse.

Marwood kept halting mid-monologue, complaining that his best passages had been cut.

Clara Lovick, playing one of the Queen's attendants, contrived to spill a jug of wine down Abby's robe.

Two of the walk-ons, feigning discourse, suddenly argued loudly, then broke into fisticuffs. One fell backwards into a prop pillar, which toppled into another, and that into its neighbour, sending players scattering.

Faybourne arrived late, trailing theatrical woe and sack fumes.

Lucius bellowed at Pip, who had missed his cue, and the poor lad fled the stage in tears.

As for Abby... It was all too much. She tried to keep her voice steady and timing precise amid such mayhem, but each attempt to step into Seraphina's skin felt more like reaching for the moon. Tresillion shouted at her for rushing, then for dragging, until eventually he gave up altogether, announcing it was time for supper.

The writer, Jack Sawyer, sat stock still at the front of the pit, head in hands. He might well have seen a ghost.

Chapter Twenty-Seven

The Royal Box

Abby wanted to run from the King's Playhouse and never again darken its doors. She was no actor, and had fooled herself into thinking she was equal to the deception. Neither, it seemed, was she much of an inquisitor. She may have lately wheedled from Faybourne the names of several King's Company shareholders, but she was no closer to uncovering Franny Jenkins's murderer.

Perhaps as punishment for the morning's dire performances, Tresillion did not lead them to The Cock for supper, but sent a minion to fetch food from a local cookhouse.

When she was handed a cold pie that smelled of eel - or offal, it was hard to tell - she stared at it for a while, fighting the lump rising in her throat, then tossed it into a corner. Hungry as she was, having foregone breakfast, she had no appetite for food.

The tiring-house had become subdued, reflecting the general malaise. The principal actors were absent, no doubt sulking in their tiring-rooms, and the walk-ons were gathered in a gang, collectively moping.

Seeing no ally, Abby slipped through the curtain into one of the wings, and found herself on the apron, quite alone.

She seated herself at the front of the stage, feet dangling over the recessed musicians' gallery, and stared up into the house. So many seats. Empty now – yet tomorrow…

Out of the corner of her eye, she caught movement, high and to her left.

There, in a box draped with colourful banners and topped with the King's crest, she saw Orange Bess busying herself with a cloth beside a tall gilded throne.

Having had no chance to explore, Abby quickly became disoriented amid the maze of stairways and passages leading upwards to the various sections of the auditorium. Navigating the narrow, mildewed steps and ill-lit timbers reminded her of plunging into the bowels of the HMS Venturer, back when she, Pepys and Jacob had been pursuing the Plague Doctor.

How she longed for their company now.

Mistakenly, she emerged first into the lower gallery, to see Bess still working in the royal box, on the same level but far off into the wing. Building a map in her mind, she headed back into the staircases and soon found herself confronted by a latched oaken door, bearing the same royal crest she had seen from the stage.

This must be it, she thought.

The padlock, she noticed, had been left open.

When Abby stepped through a pair of heavy curtains into the royal box, Bess all but jumped out of her skin.

"Oh my goodness!" the old woman exclaimed, retrieving her fan from the floor and wafting it furiously. "I thought 'twas the ghost of the Lord Protector himself! But you ain't half as ugly." She exhaled lustily. "So, tell old Bess. What brings you up here?"

The kindness in her voice almost broke Abby's resolve. She tried to answer but no words came.

Bess stepped forward and enveloped her in a soft embrace. "Not going to plan, eh? Well, don't you fret. Ain't nobody else faring much better. The day before's ever thus. Too many moths in the tummy."

Abby studied her pale green eyes, seeking the truth.

The wily old bird caught her despairing look. "On my oath, duck, I'll never forget the eve of The Merry Gallows in 'ere. Trapdoor jammed with Faybourne half in, half out. They had to oil the hinges wi' goose fat to wrest him free! Then one of the flying Gods dropped on the fellow playing the angel. House in uproar - *purse full o' coin.* We had a ball. Mayhem today means a miracle on the morrow, you mark Orange Bess's words."

Abby could not help but smile. "What are you doing up here, Bess, in the King's box?"

The old woman held up a cloth. "Like to give His Majesty's throne a polish, don't I? Nearest I'll ever come to the royal backside." She chuckled.

As far as Abby could see, the place already looked spotless. "I thought you sold oranges?"

"Sell all sorts. I lend a hand where I can. Busy bee, see?"

Abby consciously bit her lower lip. "Perhaps you can help me?"

Bess released her grip and stepped back. "Thought I already had."

"What know you of Edmund Fletcher?"

"Why d'you ask? I know that rogue well enough. All bluster 'n' breeches, I'd say. Likes to puff hisself up, but I've his measure."

Abby sucked in her cheeks. "You don't think he's responsible for…"

"Franny's murder?" Bess wiped her nose with the back of her hand. "How? He don't belong here."

"What if he sent an assassin?" Abby asked, Hook-Hand in mind.

Bess screwed up her face, which only deepened her wrinkles. "Well, the rivalry turned nasty when lovely Benedict left, but…"

"You told me you had a suspect in mind?"

"Ain't had no time to do me own investigating, have I? Good heavens, girl! Give me a moment."

"I heard…"

Bess sighed and wagged a finger. "You hear too much, my duck. Been hearin' tales 'bout you asking too many questions. Folks is growin' suspicious, an' you don't want that."

Abby felt her cheeks burn, but chanced her luck. She could trust the old woman, she felt. "I heard you held shares," she said. "In the company."

Chuckling bumptiously, Bess selected an orange from her apron and began polishing it on her sleeve. "'Tis an open secret here. You don't know who I am, do you?"

As she spoke, Abby noticed the actors filing back onto the stage below, several already dressed for their parts. Horror-struck, she threw her hands to her mouth.

Bess followed her gaze. "You'd best get on, missy, or there'll be hell to pay."

As Abby turned, Bess tossed her the orange with the words, "Here, take this. Make you strong."

But the inquisitor was not ready. It bounced off her hand, struck the edge of the balcony, and plummeted into the pit, landing with an echoing *squelch*.

All eyes sought the royal box.

"May we trouble you for your attention, Mistress Harcourt?" Tresillion called up, his tone dripping sarcasm.

Then, to his assembled cast, loud enough for her to hear, he added, "Had I an understudy, she would be playing the part."

Chapter Twenty-Eight

Choice of Three

Despite holding one of the leading roles, Abby was consigned to the walk-ons' communal tiring-room, even though Franny Jenkins's now stood empty. Out of respect for the freshly deceased actor, she reasoned. Or perhaps pompous Peregrine Marwood had conspired with Tresillion to ensure she knew her place?

A couple of walk-ons were already inside as she pushed through the curtain door. One was wrestling with a boot strap, the other painting on a fake battle scar. Discoursing on art and its nobility, they cast her nary a glance.

Against the far wall was a long, narrow table lined with stools, sputtering candles and looking glasses. Its surface was strewn with combs, pots of rouge and ceruse, wig stands, powder puffs, a stray snuff box, a tiny painted family portrait and a half-eaten apple. The floor was cluttered with baskets brimming with crumpled clothing, and open chests spilling over with props and theatrical detritus. Around the walls, unused attire hung from nails.

Abby spotted her white Queen's robe and, thankful to see the walk-ons leaving, hurriedly dressed.

She was down to her linen shift when the curtain bulged and Pip appeared, clad in his soldier's uniform. Gasping, she crossed her arms over her chest.

He looked more put out than she did.

"What's the matter?" he asked, brow knitted.

And she realised: actors, especially the walk-ons, would be used to dressing alongside one other, men and women alike. She was giving herself away.

"Oh, nought," she said, reaching for her robe as nonchalantly as she could manage.

Pip threw himself onto a stool and grabbed the snuff box. "You're late," he said. "They've started."

Flicking open the lid, he pinched a generous dose of the brown powder between thumb and forefinger. Abby noticed his hand was shaking.

"You're nervous," she said, frantically pulling on a shoe.

He glared, the dark rings under his eyes lending his pristine features a wearied tone.

"I meant, I am too!" she added quickly. The last thing she needed was upset one of her precious few allies.

Returning to his snuff, Pip threw back his head and inhaled sharply. Moments later, he let out a delicate, almost effeminate sneeze. The scent of bergamot lingered in the air.

"Isn't Bess a treasure?" he said.

Abby clasped her hands together. "I think I love her!"

It was how she imagined an actor might respond, and she was pleased with it.

Pip dabbed at his nostrils with a handkerchief. "What did you speak of?"

Is he suspicious of me? she wondered. She had been asking too many questions, and would need to play her cards closer to her chest in future.

She dodged his question. "I love her so much," she said, pulling the robe over her head and adding as she emerged, "that I wish she were my mother."

Pip snorted. "You're too late," he said, snapping the snuff box shut and rising. "She's already Mr Tresillion's. Come! We're late."

If anything, the day's second rehearsal played out more chaotically than the first, though Abby could console herself that her performance was no worse than that of several seasoned actors.

Matters were not helped by the musicians, newly arrived and unfamiliar with the play. They were tentatively feeling their way through the score, and some were clearly improvising.

Trumpet fanfares for grand entrances arrived too early or too late, throwing the actors off their marks. Viols and violins clashed, hautboys honked, and the fellow on the tabor - who was drunk - left his seat and began marching around the auditorium, thinking himself in some sort of parade. He was bundled outside, howling profanities, by Tibbet and a couple of attendants.

It took its toll on the company. Lucius entered the stage on Marwood's cue, and the sparring actors had to be prised apart. Pip continually fluffed his lines and looked frankly terror-struck, scratching all the while at a growing red rash on his arm. And Tresillion sat staring, mute and all but defeated, haranguing poor Jack Sawyer, as if the whole sorry debacle were his fault.

Much of it went over Abby's head, so preoccupied was she by the prospect of being suspended a few dozen feet in the air, on a rickety pulley mechanism. It was not lost on her that the scene involved her meeting Fate himself.

She was petrified.

But there was no escaping the scene, a dramatic denouement to the entire production, unprecedented on a London stage.

As Tresillion had told her, "You'll rise higher than any actor ever dared, and London will talk of nought else for a week."

Concealed from the house in one wing, Tibbet attached Abby to the rope that would haul her into the heavens. As he fiddled with the knots at her back, she gazed upward at the wide pulley wheel, high among the rafters. It seemed improbably far away.

Her thick woollen robe had a leather harness sewn inside. A short Y-shaped rope linked her to the winching line; its two lower ends were fastened beneath her shoulders, and the upper tied to the line itself.

Way up in the heavens, a man waited with the counterweight, ready to release it on cue. Back in the wings, another held the trailing end of the rope, drawing it in or letting it out to raise or lower Queen Seraphina, then tying it off when she reached her mark.

Abby noticed she was trembling. "You've done this before?" she asked Tibbet.

"Many times," he said. "You're just goin' higher."

She let out a little wail. "How do you even see your knots? 'Tis so dark here."

"Would you rather the audience see us?"

"If it means you tying a knot that holds, then aye, very much!"

He grunted. "Told yer, I've had better actors'n you flyin'. Could do it blindfolded."

"Are we set?" called Tresillion.

"Aye, sir!" came Tibbet's reply.

With a hefty, testing tug on the harness that near pulled Abby off her feet, he turned, making for the auditorium.

Tresillion nodded towards his three principal actors. "Spirits?"

"Just get on with it!" Marwood huffed, donning his mask.

Abby gazed out at the Spirits of Power, Love and Folly, onstage in their silken robes of purple, red and pale grey. Masked, they stood within a circle of tall candelabras, each bearing a dozen tiny flames. The backdrop - a deep-blue cloth painted with golden stars - hung high behind them, while the side shutters depicted cherubs, peeking out, awaiting the Queen's fate.

The wintry ring of a handbell jolted Abby from her reverie. It was the cue for the scene to begin.

Frantically, she tried to remember her next line. Her entire body was quaking now, and she felt disembodied, as if watching herself from above.

Power: Is that my Queen arriving yonder?
Love: Heart-bound, and heavy with choice.
Folly: Or giddy with it, I'll favour.

Stepping from the wings, Abby felt herself compelled forward by some unseen force, toward the low platform on which she would stand. In a daze, she glimpsed faces in the opposite wing, craning to eye her progress.

You'll rise higher than any actor ever dared, she repeated inwardly, losing herself in the mantra.

A drum roll urged her up the three steps onto the platform, shrouded in white. As she did so, the harness tightened beneath her arms, as the man in the heavens took up the slack.

Gazing out into the auditorium, which seemed to her veiled behind gauze, she raised her arms, letting her shimmering sleeves unfurl like wings.

As she did so, there came a commotion from the side of the stage - elbowing and grumbling among the clustered spectators - and young Pip lurched onto the stage, aiming insults at whoever had pushed him.

Lucius ripped off his mask, face creased in fury. "Young fool! Get off! Get off! You're not fit to grace the King's stage!"

Aghast, Pip pressed back into the crowd.

Abby forced herself to block it out. "I submit myself to judgement and embrace Fate's most righteous path!" she heard herself call out.

The words sounded muffled.

The harness began to bite beneath her arms, though she felt no pain.

Her feet grew weightless. She looked down.

Already a foot from the platform, she was rising. Not smoothly, but in rhythmic jolts, each pull sending a shudder through her slight frame.

It was all she could do not to panic. Resolutely, she held her arms wide, her silken wings wafting with each movement, allowing the ropes bear her upward.

Stringed instruments soared.

Power: Lo! She climbs, as once she did, when sceptre and treaty first bowed her gentle form.

Love: Lo! She climbs, forsaking state's cruel trappings for her one heart's true desire.

Folly: Lo! She climbs, to trade a crown for a kiss... or for nought at all.

Higher Abby rose, as the single sharp *doomp* of a kettle drum rang out.

Thunder crashed – somewhere below, a great copper sheet was set trembling.

It was Fate, calling.

Without warning, her ascent halted. She began swaying gently, side to side, and did not dare look down.

The silence was absolute, as if all the theatre had become blanketed with snow.

A voice rang out. "Who summons me past duty..."

She recognised the line. It was written on her cue roll.

My line! she realised, with a jolt that sent her bouncing. *The prompter!*

Suddenly, she became aware of the creaking of the rope and the pain beneath her arms.

Inhaling deeply, she steeled herself. "Who summons me past duty? I have ruled, and I have yielded. I have worn the crown, yet worn it hollow. Now tell me true. What fate shall follow, should I forsake my realm?"

The kettle drum began to rumble, low and ominous. The Spirits lifted their gaze.

Power: Choose power and govern unbound!
Love: Choose love and dwell unthroned!
Folly: Choose neither, and see me dance!

The drum's rumble built to a fury. Abby's next cue.

"Or what if I choose none of you? Neither crown, nor love, nor folly? But choose the space between? I choose freedom! What say you, Fate?"

Silence.
Fate, uncertain now, defeated.
The three Spirits backed away, fading into shadows.
Abby's Seraphina let out a triumphant, joyous laugh. "So be it! If Fate is no king of mine, then I shall be Queen of my own destiny!"

"Bravo!" Abby heard. Then another.

She dared to look down.

Tresillion was there, small as a toy figure, on his feet. It was his voice she had heard. Sawyer's, too.

The Spirits, unmasked, returned to the stage. Lucius was clapping like a man possessed. Faybourne joined in, more begrudgingly. Marwood, not at all.

Those clustered in the wings emerged to show their appreciation.

As the rope was lowered, Abby felt suffused by a golden glow.

Then came the cry, booming and delirious, rolling toward the stage from somewhere deep within the darkened house.

"How dare you, sir!"

Chapter Twenty-Nine

No Sailor

"How dare you, sir!" It came again.

Still some dozen feet above her platform, Abby peered out into the murk and saw him.

She knew him instantly - he had darkened her dreams - and began struggling, kicking her legs, desperate to escape the harness that dangled her aloft, trapping her on strings like a marionette.

"Set me down! Set me down!"

That devil had seen her cast out of his house, on the same street where her father had died. He had hired a cur with a hook for a hand to terrorise an innocent family, setting in motion the chain of events that had brought fiery ruin upon the City of London.

That devil was Edmund Fletcher.

"Set me down at once!"

The manager of the Duke's Company barged through the gate into the pit with such wild abandon that he clattered against both sides. That was when Abby saw it: the sword.

She had made it to the floor and was now imploring somebody - anybody - to untie her from the harness.

"Tibbet!" she hollered in desperation, only to spot him down in the pit, barring Fletcher's advance.

Next, she felt hands tugging at her knots. She turned to find Lucius, blissful and unruffled.

"Can't have a handsome maiden bound before a monster," he said with a wink.

She returned a broken smile.

When her gaze slid to the pit, Tibbet, club in hand, was squaring off against the sword-wielding Fletcher.

"You shall not pass," he told him, feet set, club raised.

Fletcher extended his sword arm. He wore gold-trimmed green beneath a floppy black hat, and polished spurs protruded from his high leather boots. Most striking of all was his moustache: extravagantly primped and long out of fashion, in auburn streaked with grey.

"Out of my, Tibbet. My quarrel's not with you. My quarrel…" He swivelled, thrusting the point of his sword towards Tresillion. "…is with that thieving cur. And his poxy lap-dog. What say you, Thomas? Mr Sawyer?"

The poor author was cowering across his bench, trying vainly to tunnel his way out of sight.

Without warning, Fletcher broke left, hurtling between rows of benches, then turned and began leapfrogging them in a bid to reach his quarry. Tibbet set off after him, until Fetcher upended a bench in his path and he caught it with a trailing foot, sprawling flat on his face.

Lucius, clearly no former sailor, was still struggling with Abby's knots. Nobody else was rushing to Tresillion's aid, preferring instead to gawp and gossip.

Fletcher reached his rival, panting, a single bench now between them.

He flashed his blade toward Tibbet. "Keep your nose out, man."

Then he leaned over the bench to peer at the cowering Sawyer, and jabbed him with his sword-tip. The quailing soul squealed like a hunted boar. Fletcher reached down, seized him by the collar, and hauled him over the bench.

"My property, I believe," he said.

Tresillion stiffened, hooking his thumbs into his lapels. There was no escaping he was half Fletcher's size. "You can have him, Edmund. Just as you took Lansmere. It matters not. Mr Sawyer's work here is done."

Fletcher sheathed his sword. "I watched your closing scene from the back of your house, Thomas. Who's your new Franny? I fancy the King'll need new breeches when he sets eyes on her."

He already has, thought Abby, turning to glare at the fumbling Lucius, who responded with a show of gleaming teeth and a sheepish shrug.

Fletcher grabbed Sawyer by the scruff of the neck and began hauling him from the theatre.

At the threshold, he turned. "This isn't over, Thomas. I'll not forget your treachery. As surely as the Duke's Company is the finest in the land, so your company will perish."

"Do your worst, Edmund," Tresillion called back, waving him away with gloved fingers.

"Oh, believe me. I shall."

With that, Edmund Fletcher was gone.

"At last!" Lucius exclaimed, stepping back from his work. "That second knot was a devil."

If he was expecting Abby's gratitude, none came.

She was already off, hot on her nemesis' heels.

Chapter Thirty

Nemesis

Hindered by Sawyer's wriggling, Fletcher had barely turned left onto Bridges Street when Abby caught up with him. Her robe, with all its internal strapping, was bulky and awkward, and she ground gratefully to a halt.

"Edmund Fletcher," she gasped.

He turned and raised a bushy eyebrow. "'Tis you," he said, somewhat startled. "The new Franny. I don't believe I have had the pleasure."

"Oh, you have, sir. You have."

London was alive now, at dusk. Hackney coaches and sedan chairs made their way west to Covent Garden and south toward the river. The creak of wheels and the exhortations of hawkers on corners filled the pungent, smoky air. Linkboys paced ahead of their wealthy employers, their torches sputtering, while beggars stirred in shadows, pleading for coin or crust. Couples passing by left behind lingering traces of exotic scent.

Abby noticed none of it.

Fletcher stepped forward, expecting to take her hand for a kiss. Instead, she pulled back.

His emerald eyes narrowed.

Seizing his chance, Sawyer made a break for it on long strides. Too long, as it turned out, since he stumbled, careened into a wall, and collapsed in a heap. Ladies in lace petticoats stepped over him, as if he were just another drunk.

"Have we met before?" Fletcher asked.

"Indeed we have." Nervy and restless, she smoothed her robe. "At your house by The Clink."

He pushed out his lower lip. "I believe I would remember one so handsome as you. What, pray, is your name, mistress?"

When he moved forward, she again retreated.

He chuckled, but uncertain. "Your eyes… are exquisite. I…"

"My name is Abigail Harcourt. I am personal inquisitor to Mr Samuel Pepys. I believe you know him?"

All Fletcher's charm evaporated. "That egregious philanderer! If I…" He stopped, studying her. "Hold a while. I *do* remember you. You came to my house with that gangling clodpot… What was his name?"

"Jacob Standish."

He slapped a fist into his palm. "Jacob Standish!"

"You had me thrown out."

"I did! I recall it now." He seemed almost jovial, relishing the memory.

Abby licked her chill lips. "You referred to me as 'wretch'."

He gazed upwards, twirling his moustache between finger and thumb. "Did I now? Then how the blazes have you come…" he paused, recollecting, "but three months later, to…"

"*Four months*," she cut in, laced with venom. "I can tell you the precise date we first met."

"How so? Since it escapes me entirely."

"The terrible fire started that very same night, on Pudding Lane."

"Terrible indeed. But that we might…"

"Be silent!" she snapped, startling him.

He raised a hand as if to strike her, full of menace.

Again, she pulled back, but refused to be subsumed by his power. The last time they met, she had fled his house in tears. It had stung ever since. The knowledge of what he did - the unholy catastrophe he had set in motion - would not… would never leave her.

She longed for justice. And here was her chance.

"You started that fire, Mr Fletcher, whether you lit the first flame or not."

Lowering his hand, he shook his head, staring as if she had lost her mind.

So she reminded him. "You know Henry Trevelyan?"

He managed a single nod, more a droop of the head.

"You sent him to William Baxter's house on Pudding Lane. You believed he'd stolen Mr Pepys's diaries, in which my…" She almost used 'master'. "In which my employer had, you believed, recounted an illicit liaison with your wife, Beatrix."

A rumble was growing somewhere inside Edmund Fletcher. Somewhere deep down.

Despite feeling nauseous, Abby continued. "If the diaries were stolen, you feared blackmail or worse - ruin - so sent Trevelyan, your henchman, to retrieve them."

She saw in Fletcher's blazing eyes that her words were true.

"Unable to find the diaries, since Mr Baxter never had them, Trevelyan burned down their house on Pudding Lane. 'Twas the second day of September, 1666."

With a roar, Fletcher lunged. Grabbing fistfuls of her robe, he lifted her off her feet, bringing their faces close. A whimper escaped her lips, and she hated herself for it.

She smelled cinnamon on his moustache, and tobacco on his breath. The whites of his eyes had turned crimson.

"If I am such a monster," he snarled, spittle foaming in the corners of his mouth, "then heed well these words, impudent *wretch*: tomorrow, when you are ascended into the heavens, your precious playhouse shall burn." He sneered. "And no more shall be your slander."

"But the King," she managed, in all but a whisper.

He threw her to the ground. Passers-by stared, but did not stop.

Fletcher turned, saw that Sawyer was gone, and loped away toward the river.

Chapter Thirty-One

To Dare

After being so cruelly shunned by the Cockpit's manager, Edmund Fletcher set about poaching players from Beeston's companies. Disgruntled understudies, and overlooked journeymen who felt they deserved more.

Edmund promised them the earth, if only they would share his vision. Few did. Only the sight of his money persuaded a handful to join his lowly company of St Giles Men. (The name - a sly dig at his father - tickled him.)

They performed illegally in tavern cellars, shuttered halls and stinking barns, playing to ribald audiences barely numbering in the dozens. One by one, the disillusioned players drifted back to Beeston's fold.

Edmund's petition to the Master of the Revels, Sir Henry Herbert, requesting licence to stage performances as the St Giles Men, was dismissed with scorn. The lad was barely eighteen; he had no patron and no playhouse. He would do better to mind his schooling, Herbert told him, than to chase the grandeur of men twice his age.

When, in 1638, Beeston died, Edmund dared hope it might mark a turning point. His company's ranks swelled, and with Beeston's theatres in disarray while a successor was appointed, the St Giles Men made something of a name for themselves.

Yet it was not to be. Soldiers broke up their performances and, in time, Edmund was arrested.

His six months in Bridewell gaol were the most miserable of his life.

When he emerged into London's festering streets – a dull drizzle and the stench of ordure – he was near broke after a paying a hefty fine. For a time, chastened and enfeebled, he considered abandoning his dream.

Two events reversed his fortunes.

Reduced to solo vignettes, mocked and pelted with scraps, one day he heard a lone figure applauding. Her name was Beatrix Winnick, and she smiled self-consciously as their eyes met.

They were married that autumn, one dawn in a parish church, with only the clerk and sexton to witness it. No feast nor finery. Thereafter, the wan young woman with golden ringlets and downcast gaze became his anchor and his apologist.

A year later, Civil War broke out. The Long Parliament banned stage-plays. To God-fearing, law-abiding theatrical companies, it was a death knell that would sound for years.

To Edmund Fletcher, it rang like a challenge.

If nobody held a licence, then the field was levelled.

For a while, many ignored Parliament's ban, leading to harsher penalties and greater sanction. Far from being defeated, Edmund redoubled his efforts, staging plays in cellars, yards and attics.

He recruited men like himself to the St Giles Men. Men brimming with indignation, who saw Parliament's attempts at censure as an assault upon their liberty, even their dignity.

He employed scouts to warn of soldiers' approach, and bribed officials to turn a blind eye. As the competition gradually dwindled, his coffers swelled. Royalists and bored noblemen paid good money for private entertainment behind closed doors. It raised two fingers at Cromwell's puritanical zeal.

Only those who dared might triumph.

And Edmund surely dared.

During the ensuing years of Cromwell's Protectorate, he felt invincible. They had come for him once by moonlight – at his home on Drury Lane, as Beeston's had been – and powerful friends had secured his release. Why, he had even been introduced to Lord Protector himself, who merely cast him a wary smile. As he knew full well, Cromwell was not above the odd hypocrisy.

Even so, he did not chance his head by offering a private performance.

The Civil Wars had ceased, but unrest only grew. Once angered by the King's abuse of power, the people now turned their ire upon the puritanical yoke of the Protectorate.

Cromwell's days were numbered, and Edmund bided his time.

When Charles returned from exile in France to retake his rightful throne, Edmund's name was known through all London. His defiance of Cromwell brought him to the King's attention, and swiftly into his favour.

In stark contrast to his predecessor, Charles thrived on courtly diversions and the frivolity of leisure. He adored performance and set about rejuvenating London's fallow theatre. There would be two great playhouses, he declared, and women, long shunned from the stage, would now grace it in all their beauty.

Two patents were granted by His Majesty for the operation of these playhouses.

One went to Thomas Tresillion, a trusted friend and ally, who was son of Sir Robert Tresillion, noted courtier and patron of the Arts.

The other was granted to Edmund Fletcher.

It was his finest hour. He considered disinterring his father, to have him witness the rising walls of his magnificent Lincoln's Inn Fields Theatre.

Edmund wanted for but one thing: an heir.

He loved Beatrix - how could he not? - yet her timidity galled him deeply. How could this woman, who had stood beside him even as armed men hammered on their door, dissolve into tears at his first harsh words?

In company, too, she grew diaphanous - the same woman who had bared her teeth while they plotted his success well into the night.

She worshipped him, and he, her. In rare moments of reflection, he wondered whether he showed it.

He simply was not that man, he reasoned. Blind faith, an impenetrable will, and a temper that had cowed many a fierce opponent - these had won him the splendid, coveted life he now shared with his wife. Not soft words and half-truths.

All has asked for was a son. Even a daughter might have placated him.

Yet Beatrix remained barren.

How it gripped and perplexed him.

Chapter Thirty-Two

Home

Pepys would not have it. "Gentlemen of Mr Fletcher's standing are wont to exaggerate, Abigail. It is a means by which to make themselves heard, and perfectly excusable in such circumstances. Mr Fletcher is..."

"Sir." Abby took a deep breath. "He threatened to burn down the King's Playhouse tomorrow, His Majesty and all."

Pepys smiled. "Mr Edmund Fletcher is patentee of the theatrical company of the very Duke himself – *who is the King's brother*. The chances of him setting alight the King's Playhouse are more remote than..." He drummed the arm of his chair, hunting for a metaphor, and eventually gave up. "Than the chances are of him setting alight all London."

Abby drilled her fingers into her hair. "But he did precisely that, sir! Or rather, he caused it."

They had been here before.

Pepys folded his hands into his lap. "I wish to know your progress in the investigation of Franny Jenkins's murder."

It was an end to the matter.

Abby shot Jacob a glance, which he studiously avoided.

The three were back at Jacob's townhouse. Abby had stayed there so often of late that it was beginning to seem more like home than her own little apartment. She longed to return; she missed her personal touches, dank and dingy as the place was.

But first, she had this perplexing mystery to solve, tangled with too many suspects and too many motives. If only she could narrow it down.

The day had been tumultuous, as she explained to Pepys and Jacob.

Firstly – it felt like an age ago – she had learned of Faybourne's shareholding. It was smaller than Lucius's and Marwood's, which riled him, as did the fact that Bess held one too.

"Bess?" Jacob spluttered. "Orange Bess?"

"Aye, she's Tresillion's mother," she said matter-of-factly.

Jacob's eyes widened. "That insolent old wench?"

Pepys reached for his wine, shaking his head. "I had my suspicions. Who was it, now? Aye, 'twas the Duke of Richmond who told me of some politic at the Playhouse, that Bess was rumoured to be kin to another there. I pressed him, and he turned tight-lipped. Tresillion wished it kept quiet, the Duke told me, lest it stir a hornet's nest." He took a gulp. "I now understand why."

It was Bess, Abby explained, who had told her of Benedict Lansmere's defection, and how it had soured the once-friendly rivalry between the King's and Duke's Companies. Some, like Bess and Tibbet, had spoken warmly of the man. Certain others – Lucius, who had played his understudy – appeared to loathe him.

Bess had also hinted that she harboured suspicions of the murderer's identity.

Both men shifted in their seats.

"Who?" Jacob asked.

"She wouldn't say. Told me she was wary of naming someone falsely, said she needed more time."

"When will you know?" Pepys asked.

"I pressed her on it, while she was cleaning the royal box. She told me she hadn't had the time." Abby hesitated. "I'll ask her again tomorrow."

To her mind, her most telling discovery was that Edmund Fletcher was more dangerous than even she had imagined. Wisely, she did not mention it.

Instead, she described the pervading sense of disorder at the theatre, which threatened at any moment to descend into calamity.

"The afternoon's rehearsal couldn't have fared much worse, had the roof caved in," she said.

Jacob picked up Pepys's wine, realised his mistake, replaced it and selected his own. "Yet you told us your flying scene was a triumph?"

Abby allowed herself a grin. "Aye. The only one. And that, too, was ruined by the arrival of…" She trailed off.

"Then we are set for a catastrophe tomorrow?" said Pepys.

If Fletcher isn't stopped, aye, Abby thought.

Pepys stayed up far longer than Abby had hoped. She itched to speak with Jacob alone, and longed for her bed. Tomorrow, she would play before the King - and hope to save his life.

At last, having upended the second carafe of Haut Brion, to find it empty, her employer excused himself.

Once his footsteps had faded and the latch clicked shut on his guest-chamber door upstairs, she dropped into the seat beside Jacob, lately vacated by Pepys. The fire was dying, and she felt the beginnings of a headache.

Reaching across, she gripped Jacob's knee.

"Aye," he said, before she could even speak.

It took her by surprise. "Aye, what?"

"Aye, I'll visit the Duke's Playhouse for you."

She beamed. *The old crew.* How she missed it.

"What am I to look for?" he asked.

"Break into Fletcher's office…"

"*What?*" A creak came from upstairs, and Jacob jolted. "What?" he repeated, this time in a stage whisper.

"You must find some evidence to implicate Edmund Fletcher."

"In murder? But I cannot see it."

"Who knows what he's capable of, Jacob? There'll be something sorely amiss there, I feel it. And find it, you must. Speak also with Lansmere while you're there. I'll wager he knows something we don't." She squeezed his knee. "I'm counting on you."

He swallowed. "Aye. I know it."

Chapter Thirty-Three

Calamity

Abby woke later than she hoped, the lack of sleep taking its toll on her exhausted mind and body. She slipped out of Strand Lane into a light mist, just as the first stirrings could be heard in the rooms above.

In her haste to reach the theatre, knowing preparations for the royal performance would begin in the early hours, she did not notice the figure pressed into the doorway opposite, silently watching her leave.

The moment she entered the King's Playhouse, she knew something was amiss. The people were there, as she had anticipated, but the familiar thrum of activity was absent. From behind the curtained door of the walk-ons' tiring-room, she could hear the sound of someone sobbing.

Matt Tibbet walked past her like a man in a trance.

She stopped him. "What is it? What's happened?"

And he told her.

"Orange Bess is dead."

The old woman's body lay among the vacant stools in the musician's gallery, just beneath the recessed apron. Marwood was there, and Lucius too, standing among a knot of walk-ons and attendants, gazing in mute revulsion.

Protruding from Bess's back was a silver dagger, its hilt inlaid with rubies.

Taking a deep breath, Abby knelt beside the corpse. Jacob, with his keen eye, was the inquisitor for such tasks. In his absence, she would have to suffice.

Bess's sleeves were smeared with dust and cobwebs, her eyes wide open, and her splayed hands were cut. *Did she try to fight off her attacker?* Abby wondered.

Bess was a feisty soul. It seemed likely.

Reaching out, she ran a finger over the dagger's handle.

"They're not real," came a voice from behind her, "them rubies."

"Aye," said another. "Another poor lass sent to her maker by one of Tibbet's props."

As discontent spread, Abby turned.

The faces were stony, bar Lucius's, whose lips betrayed the hint of a smirk.

Appalled, Abby snapped, "Mr Lucius!"

He started. "Forgive me, I was miles away."

Marwood scowled at him.

"Tibbet should hang for this," someone said, to a smattering of approval.

"'T'int him," another countered. "It'll be that Faybourne. Never trusted 'im. Tiny eyes."

That theory, too - meagre as it was - had its supporters.

Sensing the first stirrings of a lynch mob, Abby pushed herself to her feet.

"Everybody!" she called, raising her palms in an appeal for calm.

Before she could continue, a squat man wearing a carpenter's apron spoke up. "Who's she, then?"

"Been asking questions, I heard."

"Aye, I heard that, an' all."

"Ain't she Franny's replacement? The one playing the Queen?"

"Won't be no Queen. Won't be no play. Not after this."

A sharp clap resounded about the house, and every head turned.

Thomas Tresillion was striding along the front of the apron. His pale skin looked tauter than ever, but his eyes were glinting.

He stopped at the little group, gazed down at his dead mother, closed his eyes slowly, then faced them. "Did I hear tell there would be no play?" He waited for no reply. "That would be a tragedy, I say, in a house that has seen more than its share of late. The King shall not be denied.

The play will go on. My dear, sweet mother would have wished it."

Without another glance at Bess, he headed toward the tiring-house, rubbing his hands as he went.

"Well," said Lucius, once he was out of earshot. "You heard the gentleman."

"Still wants his takings," someone muttered. "No matter poor Bess, here."

Marwood gave a short, sardonic laugh. "Would that I saw my due share of it."

"Aye," came a chorus of replies.

Abby was shocked by their number.

Something was beginning to niggle at her. Something she may have missed, or overlooked, but could not quite place.

It would come to her in time, she told herself – yet time was a precious commodity.

Chapter Thirty-Four

Deception

Mr Pepys had an appointment at his office with the Duke Of York, and left shortly after Jacob heard Abby close the main door behind her. He had taken a swift breakfast of cold turkey pie, and assured the inquisitor he would breathe not a word of Abby's wild accusations regarding Mr Fletcher to the King's brother.

"It would not suit me well," were his parting words to her.

Jacob, too, was keen to begin the day. He missed Abby's company, which was rarely less than enlightening, and he longed to rediscover the cut and thrust of their investigations.

While she was risking life and liberty at the King's Playhouse, all to bolster Mr Pepys's standing with His Majesty, he had been shopping with Mrs Pepys.

A pleasant and lively woman, for sure, but - oh! - how she delighted in spending her husband's coin. Indeed, so profligate had she been among the perfumed stalls and galleries of the New Exchange, Jacob wondered whether Pepys might have wronged her in some way and was being held to ransom for it.

It had made him question the joys of marriage.

Still, today he felt invigorated. Abby needed him, and it renewed his sense of purpose.

An inquisitor once again, he would not let her down.

A faint dusting of frost covered The Strand, and the air was cold but still. The local butcher, setting up his display outside the shop, waved. Windows glowed, and folk hunched against the cold wandered past, this way and that.

To Jacob's left, the bells of St Clement Danes struck six, followed closely by the chime of St Mary-le-Strand. Their clangs were as familiar to Jacob as his feet. *Perhaps more so*, he mused.

The street was coming to life.

"Good morrow!" came the cheery voice.

Jacob had not spotted the figure crossing the road towards him, distracted as he was by his thoughts. When he saw who it was, his heart sank.

He reached for his periwig. "What do you want?"

"Come now, Mr Standish. I'm here to lend a hand."

"And how, pray, might you be of assistance to me, Will Harcourt?"

Abby's brother slapped Jacob on the upper arm, beaming. "Sore head? Too much ale last night?"

"Wine, if you must know. Haut Brion. The King's favourite."

He could not help noticing that Will had tidied himself since last they met. The unkempt stubble was gone, his breeches were clean, and his coat looked recently laundered. He had even taken to wearing a periwig - very much like Jacob's. Possibly neater.

"Where you bound?" Will asked.

"My destination is no concern of yours."

Jacob tried to push him aside, to be on his way, but Will stood firm.

"You're investigating Franny Jenkins's murder."

"Nonsense," Jacob snapped.

Will nudged him. "Aye, you are. Your face betrays you."

Jacob silently cursed his face. Abby's brother had outstayed his welcome.

Again, he tried to pass, and again, Will barred his way.

"I've no wish to play the inquisitor," said Will.

"What?"

"I said I've no wish to be an inquisitor. If that's your fear."

"You must take me for a fool. Stand aside"

This time, Jacob – taller than most, and almost a head above Will – pushed harder. Abby's brother stumbled back, and Jacob lunged past.

"'Twas ever the nature of the King's Company," Will called after him, "to muddle tragedy with farce."

Jacob stopped. "I beg your pardon?"

"'Twas ever the nature of the King's Company to muddle tragedy with farce. My friend, Mr Eversleigh, said it."

The inquisitor turned. "You know Eversleigh?"

"I print his broadsides. We're firm friends." Will watched Jacob's expression shift from irritated to intrigued, and struck with the line he had rehearsed during those lonely, bitter hours waiting in the doorway. "He knows all the talk of the King's Company."

The truth was, Edward Eversleigh barely acknowledged Will Harcourt's presence, and used his printing shop only because his prices were desperately low. The actors veered between adoration and scorn for the critic, depending on his published views of their performances. As for the secrets of the tiring-house, Eversleigh was witness to none.

Not that Jacob was to know any of that. "He knows who murdered Franny Jenkins?" he asked.

Will adjusted his periwig, as he had seen Jacob do. "Nay, Mr Standish. He would not be so bold. But..."

Jacob was back beside him in two long strides. "But what?"

"He believes he may hold a key. To solving the terrible crime."

Had Jacob been able to grow more ears, he would have done so. "What key?"

"Where are you bound?"

"For the theatre. Why?"

With a slow shake of the head, Will sucked in his lips.

"What is it?" Jacob asked, somewhat high-pitched.

"'Tis not the place Edward spoke of."

"Which place, then? Does it hold the key?"

"So he said."

"Then where is it? Tell me."

Will looked Jacob up and down. "I was sworn to secrecy."

A thought struck the inquisitor, and he cocked his head. "Why would you help me, Will Harcourt?"

But Will was prepared. "By helping you, I help my sister, for whom I wish only happiness and success. I love her most dearly." He inspected a fingernail. "If, in doing so, it might bring us closer together… Well, that would please me greatly, sir."

Jacob grabbed him by the collar. "Then tell me, damn you."

"If I do so," Will said, eyes glinting, "then I must swear you to secrecy."

How deliciously sweet is every moment of this exchange, Will thought. This plan had come to him in a flash of inspiration: *he need not solve the crime himself, but merely make Jacob appear the fool he was.* Send him on a wild goose chase, and the hapless inquisitor would be too mortified to admit he had been duped. The embarrassment alone would keep his deception safe.

"Very well…" Will hesitated, feigning reluctance. "The key, Edward said, is a…" He hovered on the last word, as if toying.

Jacob, staring into Will's dark soul, racked his mind. *Where had they been? What had he missed?*

Then it struck him. Browne's, where Abby had auditioned. "The coffee house?"

Will shook his head, lower lip protruding. He wanted Jacob to feel he had earned it.

"Nay?" Jacob frowned. *Where else? What other places had Abby mentioned?*

Hold! "The tavern?"

Will smiled coyly, offered the faintest of shrugs.

Jacob released his grip and stepped back. "It is? Am I right?"

Will chuckled. "Aye, Mr Standish, you have me. A tavern named…" Followed by another, barely perceptible pause.

"The Cock!"

"You knew it all along, sir!" Will bowed, marvelling. "I congratulate you. A fine inquisitor, indeed."

But not as fine as I shall be.

Chapter Thirty-Five

Secrets Shared

The death of Orange Bess left Abby with a heavy heart and a quandary. Now, she had two victims.

Left alone with Bess's body, while the others drifted off to the tiring-house to mourn, Abby found herself with time to think.

The methods of dispatch differed entirely – poison and dagger – yet it seemed unthinkable that the murderer were not one and the same. Two such devils in a single theatre would be catastrophic.

What, she wondered, *do the victims have in common?*

Franny was an actress, rumoured to have played a part in Benedict Lansmere's defection. She had written a note to Lucius, offering to "sink" his great rival, supposedly in exchange for Lucius's romantic attention – or so he claimed.

Public opinion, she was told, held Franny funnier than Faybourne and more popular than Lucius or Marwood.

What was it Tresillion had told her? Aye. "Franny was adored."

The principal actors surely envied her.

Bess, while no actress, was Tresillion's mother. Any attack on her was an attack on the theatre itself, and on the manager the principal actors blamed for their lack of rightful compensation. Was that Edmund Fletcher's work?

She had pushed his threat to burn the place down to the back of her mind. One quandary at a time. Pepys thought him harmless, and had favoured financial motives from the outset.

Her employer was no fool; it would be unwise to dismiss his suspicions.

Franny, she had learned, held company shares; now Bess, too. It did lend weight to Pepys's theory. Why else murder them both, unless to claim a greater share of the company spoils – assuming the takings were divided equally among the surviving holders?

Yet something else troubled Abby. Something graver.

In a company teeming with men, both victims were women.

Did her murderer bear some grudge against women?

Had he perhaps been rejected by both Franny and Bess... so different in age and appearance? It seemed unlikely.

What if he had once been wronged by another woman entirely, and nursed a hatred so festering it had turned murderous? Was Clara Lovick, Abby's great rival, next? Might *she herself* be next? What if…

Her reverie was interrupted by footsteps and a voice.

"Come quickly. This way."

Matt Tibbet was striding towards her, trailed by a couple of slouching attendants. He wrinkled his nose when he saw her.

"There," he said, pointing at Bess's body, as if it were not plain enough. "Wrap her up."

He tossed an old blanket to one of the men, then took Abby by the elbow and steered her away from the scene.

She struggled against his rough grip. "Ow, you're hurting me."

"I know your secret," he hissed. "*Inquisitor*."

His breath reeked of offal.

"And I know yours," she shot back.

He dropped her arm, wary gaze studying her face. "How so?"

She smiled slyly and said nothing. Everyone had a secret. What Tibbet's was, she had no idea.

"You'd never tell," he growled.

"Try me."

He cracked his knuckles. "Foolish words, mistress."

"Are you threatening me, Mr Tibbet?"

He seemed conflicted, but the devil in his gaze soft-ened. At last, he chuckled. "I'm as keen as the next man to see this villain hang. Your secret's safe with me."

Abby resisted the urge to gulp in air. "And yours with me."

"There's something I've to tell you." He pulled her close. "Last night, I was here late…"

"You saw Bess's murderer?"

"Nay. But I 'eard noises. Someone with no business here at that hour."

"Noises where?"

"Hard to say. All them bangs and clatters echo, don't they? But I'd swear they come from the fly gallery."

"Up in the rafters?"

He scoffed. "You're no actress, are yer? Aye, up in the rafters."

"For what possible purpose?"

He raised an eyebrow. "Hiding?"

A stark vision of Henry Trevelyan loomed in her mind. Had Fletcher sent his pet assassin?

Her heart quickened. "Did you give chase?"

"Never saw no one, did I? Then it went quiet."

One of the workers called out, "Got 'er, Matt!"

"Good work, lads," Tibbet replied, then tapped his nose at Abby. "Remember our deal."

She nodded. "I'm told you named Orange Bess as Fran-ny's murderer."

Tibbet pushed his face in hers. "Never took to the old hag."

When silence and stillness returned, Abby gazed up into the galleries, and swore she caught the faint, lingering odour of death.

This auditorium, which had once brimmed with wonder, now held only menace and fear. *And what part*, she wondered, *will Edmund Fletcher play in it all?*

Jacob would be making for the Duke's Playhouse, might even be confronting Fletcher at that very moment. Abby nodded to herself, satisfied.

She could rely on him.

Chapter Thirty-Six

The Trunk

M r Pepys had made Jacob aware of The Cock on Bow Street's reputation, so it was with some trepidation that he pushed open the door. Even at the early hour, the place resembled the inside of a chimney.

The Cock catered not only for rakes, fops and players, but for stallholders from the nearby market, and for wealthy residents - the sort who patronised both local theatres. Deviating from Abby's plan he may have been, but Jacob reassured himself he could - in Mr Pepys's words - kill two birds with one stone.

Truth be told, he shared Pepys's view of the Fletcher business. He had met the man himself, after all. A tyrant and a scoundrel, Fletcher might be, but his threat to burn down the King's Playhouse smacked of bluster. That he might be involved in an actress's murder beggared belief.

Still, Abby had the bit between her teeth and would need to be indulged.

"You come about the room?"

"What's that you say?"

"Must I spell it for you?" She scratched her head. "R-e-u-m?"

Jacob had been accosted by a fierce old woman, short but sturdy, with a tangled mop of greying auburn hair and a stare that could sink a galleon. *Oxford Kate*, he realised. He had been forewarned of her, too.

"Come about the room?" he echoed, still gathering his thoughts.

Kate looked the inquisitor up and down, squinting. "I took you for it, since you look nowt like my usual customers."

Jacob glanced around. The tavern was half-full, of braying gents and craggy traders battered by all weathers.

Kate turned back to her counter. "Timewaster, eh?"

Jacob caught her by the arm. This might be just the opportunity he needed: a chance to explore without arousing suspicion. "Aye, mistress. I have indeed… come about the room."

She slapped him playfully with the back of her hand. "Well why didn't yer say so! Foller me, then!"

Kate led Jacob to the rear of the pub, past the battered virginal Abby had seen, and up a narrow flight of stairs. So narrow, he had to turn his broad shoulders sideways.

At the top was a long corridor lined with doors, the walls streaked with smears and stains the inquisitor had no wish to interpret.

Kate opened one of the doors and ushered him inside. "Don't mind her things. No one's come to fetch 'em." She glared up at him, and he noticed one pupil oddly dilated. "You keep yer thieving mitts off, y'hear!"

"Oh, I surely shall. Whose… things are they?"

Kate crossed herself. "You know of Franny Jenkins? The actress?"

It was all Jacob could do not to let his jaw hit the floor.

A narrow, bare bed lay against one wall, its mattress sagging in the middle. Beside it was a three-legged stool and a chipped, dry washbasin. The fireplace was long-since cold. Above the mantel, an oval looking glass was fixed in place, and Jacob wondered how many times Franny had admired herself in it.

The empty room spoke of absence, like a stage once the audience had left.

At the end of the bed was a battered wooden trunk, its lid closed. Opposite stood a low chest of drawers.

He tried the chest first. The drawers rang hollow as he pulled them open, and all three proved empty.

The trunk, then.

As he tiptoed across the floorboards, Jacob pricked an ear. Through the thin walls came the sounds of men and women carousing - only the Lord knew what they were up to, so early in the day - making approaching footsteps hard to discern.

The lid creaked as he lifted it, masked by the scrabbling of a pigeon across the roof.

Inside were neatly folded clothes, with a single pewter comb laid on top. Digging a hand down, he pulled out pile after pile and set them on the floor.

At the bottom, among the personal effects - a hand mirror, playbooks, gloves, a lace-trimmed kerchief, empty drawstring purse - his eyes were drawn to a small jewellery box and a well-thumbed calf-skin notebook.

A cursory glance inside showed the jewellery box contained little of value, and Jacob found himself wondering at the worth of those much-coveted King's Company shares. A brass-framed miniature lay face-down, and he turned it over. Crude as the portrait was, Jacob recognised the subject at once. The chiselled jaw, a glimpse of white teeth.

Dorian Lucius.

He closed the jewellery box and carefully, almost reverently, replaced it. That was when he heard it, the sound he had been dreading: footsteps. Ascending.

Hurriedly, quelling a rising panic, he stuffed the notebook inside his coat, and flung the clothes back into the trunk. He had just closed the lid, when the door flew open. His face adopted a rictus grin.

Oxford Kate stood in the doorway, arms folded, expression like thunder. "What have you…?"

"I-I'll take it!" he blurted out.

Her fury evaporated, as the sound of silver dripping through fingers rang in her ears.

Chapter Thirty-Seven

Vindication

The afternoon's debut performance of The Masque of Sighs, already in disarray, teetered into something approaching farce. Several of the craftsmen, who had known Orange Bess since the days of the Commonwealth, were distracted and jittery. A carpenter drove a nail through his thumb, and a scenery flat representing Fate, lordly among clouds, was slotted into its groove upside down.

Hugh Faybourne refused to emerge from his tiring-room until the theatre was searched from top to bottom, convinced the murderer lay in wait for him.

Peregrine Marwood simply left the building.

"He'll return, as usual," said Tresillion as the rear door slammed shut, but his hollowed eyes and skewed periwig suggested a man on the edge.

Seeing all the gawping faces, he flailed his arms. "Get to work! Tidy, rehearse, prepare! The King arrives in…" Bells outside chimed the ninth hour. "Six hours! If we are to go down, we shall do so fighting. Final rehearsal at noon!"

And with a crisp clap, which caused one or two of the more fretful souls to jump, he disappeared toward his office.

Abby looked around for an ally, anybody she might speak to, but saw only unfamiliar faces absorbed in their own tasks. *What if Faybourne's right?* she thought. If Tibbet had indeed heard an intruder the night before, perhaps he remained at large?

When had Bess been killed? During those small hours, or after arriving earlier that morning?

She chided herself for not feeling the body. Had it been cold, she might have known. Jacob would have done so; of that, she was sure.

What had Bess been doing in the musicians' gallery? Had she been stabbed there, or dragged?

Confident that she knew her lines, Abby glanced about to ensure nobody was watching, and made for the last place she had seen Tresillion's mother alive: the royal box.

She found nothing. No tell-tale clue, no drips of blood, no sign of a struggle.

As she slumped over the balcony, head resting on her arms, movement below caught her eye.

From the corner of her gaze, she saw a tall man with sandy hair stoop and disappear through a door set into the far end of the apron. He was carrying a cutlass and, though she caught only a fleeting, dull glimmer as the door closed, she felt certain she glimpsed the steely curve a hooked hand.

Her chest shuddered.

Henry Trevelyan?

Abby had come face to face with Fletcher's assassin during the Plague Doctor investigation. She knew his appearance, would know him anywhere. And that man… *it was him.*

Gripped by a moment of recklessness, she half-considered vaulting the balcony. Then reason prevailed, and she spun and raced for the stairs.

She had been right all along.

Chapter Thirty-Eight

The Duke's Company

Jacob's long coat flapped behind him as he rounded Bow Street onto Russell Street. In his indecent haste, he collided full-tilt with a perfume seller, sending man and wares flying.

Seeing his assailant's expensively tailored attire, the seller swallowed the volley of abuse poised on his frost-bitten lips, and began returning the pomanders and herb bundles to his tray.

"Sweet thyme for temperance?" he called after the fleeting inquisitor.

Jacob was on a mission, and he was late.

To his surprise, Will Harcourt's urging to visit The Cock had proven fruitful. Or so he hoped.

He would inspect Franny's notebook just as soon as he dared come to a halt. The prospect of Oxford Kate discovering his meddling did not bear thinking about - nor that he had no real need of the room he had apparently just hired.

Abby had told him all she knew of the Duke's Play-house, also known as the Lincoln's Inn Fields Theatre, so named for its location. Jacob had visited the fields on occasion, escaping the house on Strand Lane and its familial reproach, and knew the theatre lay at the eastern end of Russell Street.

Only when the theatre building rose before him did he stop to gather his breath. He felt for the notebook inside his coat and gave it a reassuring pat.

What secrets will it hold? he wondered, pulling it free and feverishly flipping through its curling pages. He had played second fiddle to Abby long enough; how he longed to be the one to flourish the key that would uncover the murderer.

Inside, amid crude sketches of stage attire and the odd pressed flower, he found a sequence of dates: 2 January, 3 January, 4 January… A diary, he realised.

He had found Franny Jenkins's diary.

Yet the writing beneath each date, a curious scrawl of lines and symbols, was meaningless to him.

A code? Had the ill-fated actress written in cipher, protecting her innermost thoughts from prying eyes?

Who would do such a thing?

And then it occurred to him: Mr Pepys.

Abby had once glimpsed Pepys's dairy during her time as his maidservant, and had told Jacob about her master's strange system of shortwriting. Like Franny's, it had looked impenetrable – until she had discovered on Pepys's library shelves a slim tome titled Tachygraphy or Shortwriting: The Most Easie, Exact & Speedie, by one Thomas Shelton.

Abby never acted upon her discovery, she told Jacob. It would have meant certain dismissal, and anyway she was too loyal. But she had felt sure Shelton's cipher would unlock her master's private musings.

Was Franny's cipher the same?

Cursing his misfortune, Jacob slid the diary back inside his coat and slipped through the grand doorway of the Duke's Playhouse.

The layout of the auditorium was much like the Kings' – the familiar balconies and boxes – but the pit here was sunken, and the proscenium arch more elaborate, framed in carved wood and adorned with classical detailing.

Twin niches flanked the upper arch, each bearing a carved female figure draped in flowing folds. At the apex, high above the stage, stood the Duke of York's coat of arms, including a shield bearing the same label Jacob had seen on Franny's poisoned goblet.

Here, rich carvings and polished wood replaced the gilt leather and green baize of the King's Playhouse. It was altogether a more alluring prospect.

There were two men on the stage, each holding a cue roll, apparently rehearsing their parts. The one speaking had the most mellifluous of timbres, rich as cream.

Neither, Jacob was relieved to note, was Edmund Fletcher. He had not forgotten their last meeting, nor ever could, and was hardly relishing the prospect of their reacquaintance.

So entranced had he been by the actors' performance that a while passed before he realised it had ceased, and both men were now peering out into the auditorium.

"Is that Mr Gresham's man?" the one with the voice called out, laced with impatience. "I am Lansmere."

Jacob centred his skewed periwig. "Aye, Mr Lansmere, sir," he heard himself reply. "I am indeed Gresham's man."

Having dismissed his fellow actor, Benedict Lansmere guided Jacob toward the seats at the rear of the pit. His hushed tone suggested he was keen they were not overheard.

When they were seated, his wandering silvery eyes appraised the inquisitor. "Is this whom the Duke's Company send, to protect for me my just entitlement?" Before Jacob could stammer a reply, he went on, "Your periwig, Mr...?"

"Standish."

"Pray lower your voice, sir. Your periwig, Mr Standish, appears fashioned from woodland detritus. Have you recently vacated a hedge?"

"Nay, sir."

"Nay, sir," Lansmere replied, arching a coiffed eyebrow.

This actor, whom Lucius had replaced, bore a similar bold air. Both had features that might have been carved from marble. Perfect noses and cleft chins. Yet Lansmere was clearly the elder, his cropped dark hair greying above the ears, and fine lines etched across his forehead, no doubt from all those years of enunciating.

And he was not finished. "Then I ask you this, Mr Standish: what have you to say for yourself?"

Again, fortunately for Jacob, the question proved rhetorical.

"I have broken no clause in my contract with Tresillion. My share in his company lasts in perpetuity… Nay, sir, hold your tongue. A forked tongue, I might add. The tongue of a devil, sir."

"I…" Jacob managed.

Lansmere pressed a finger to the inquisitor's lips. "As you are undoubtedly aware, since scurrilous rumour travels faster in the theatre than locusts upon Egypt, I left the King's Company because the air there had grown… troublesome. I showed someone a kindness. Perhaps too much. It bred whispers – misunderstandings, if we are generous.

"A fool, I was. My affections misplaced. I sent letters. A trinket or two, perhaps. Yet reply, there came none. And thus, with heavy heart, I withdrew."

His voice carried a weight of sadness. "Such is frailty. And I am more frail than most. My heart was laid bare, and for what? A flight from fate. And that woman's threat."

Finally, Lansmere paused for breath, and Jacob was able to gather his wits. If his reading of the whispered rant was sound, this echoed what Matt Tibbet had suggested: that Franny Jenkins had seen something, and used it.

"Franny Jenkins…" he began.

It was all it took.

"Speak not that vile name, sir, lest my poor ears wither and drop like grapes from a vine in winter. A harlot and a scoundrel. And now," he smiled for the first time, "she lies dead. And that, sir, is why I shall not yield my rightful share. At last, I am free to spend it again."

Jacob knew he had the time it took Lansmere to fold his arms and lean back in his seat to piece it all together. Franny had indeed blackmailed him over a tryst – but with whom? And why would it lead to Lansmere's flight? Abby had mentioned a Clara somebody…

There was nothing else for it. "This assignation, sir. With whom…?"

It was as far as he got.

Lansmere's eyes bulged. "That is my business, sir!" he bellowed, all subterfuge dispensed with.

"Benedict?"

At once, Lansmere fell silent, straightened his attire, and stood. "Aye, over here."

"Who's that you're with?"

Jacob knew the voice. Though they had last met on the night of the fire, some four months ago, it still rang in his ears on dread nights.

Edmund Fletcher.

Chapter Thirty-Nine

The Hunt

Abby hurled herself down the steep, dark staircases three steps at a time, all caution flung to the wind. What she would do when she caught up with Hook-Hand - a brute twice her size, devoid of morals - she did not stop to consider.

Two painters, busy touching up flats, paused to watch her streak past the front of the stage. Her piled red hair, having lost its pin, flew behind her; it almost looked as if her head were ablaze.

"Cat got yer garter?" one of the men called after her.

At the far end of the apron, she skidded to a halt. There was the door Hook-Hand had taken, cut into the timber wall.

It had not occurred to her that the area beneath the stage might be occupied. What she expected to find there, she had no idea.

She pushed open the door and was confronted by near darkness. A single oil-lamp some distance away, set on the floor among looming shapes, cast long shadows across the space. To her left ran the north wall of the theatre; to her right, the apron wall bulged inwards to make room for the musicians' gallery.

Somewhere in the gloom ahead, she heard movement. Faint, but deliberate.

Hook-Hand.

The air was thick with dust and mildew. Cobwebs clung to her face as she passed, and the scampering of rodents echoed. The ceiling was high enough for her walk upright; Hook-Hand would have to have stooped.

Swallowing drily, she headed inside, aiming for the lamp.

She would need light to face this deadly quarry.

The closer she came, the more she could make out. Stored scenery - half a fluted column, cracked and flaking flats, great rolled backdrops - lay jumbled among coiled ropes, suspended chains and rusting pulleys.

Grateful to have reached the lamp undetected, she raised it cautiously, conscious of lighting herself up for all to see.

At the rear of the understage, below where she supposed the tiring-house must be, stood a row of half a dozen small wooden huts. All their doors were shut, bar one. Footsteps overhead masked the sound of hers, and she pressed on.

Her mind rolled back to that terrible night when London had been set ablaze. She and Jacob had returned to Pudding Lane to find the Baxters' home already alight. The unbearable heat; the panic-stricken crowd; that unnatural, hellish glow on every terrified face. Weeping children had clutched at their mothers' aprons, fearing a descent into Hell.

She and Jacob had watched as the flames leapt from one building to the next, spreading with such dreadful speed.

A sickening sense had taken hold of her: that this might be worse than all the fires that had gone before. What she would have sacrificed to be wrong.

Jacob had been so certain that William Baxter had stolen her master's diaries. As, tragically, had Edmund Fletcher, who had wheedled the information from her fellow inquisitor. She did not blame Jacob - it was their first investigation, and they had entered it blind and naive.

Baxter himself had gone to fetch the alderman, leaving his wife, Sarah, and their daughter, staring helplessly up at their engulfed home. It was Sarah who had told them of Hook-Hand.

They would later learn his name: Thomas Trevelyan, a former captain in Cromwell's navy. A good man once, whose heart had turned black.

He had come to the Baxters seeking the diaries, on Fletcher's orders. Having left empty-handed, he returned later with a flaming torch, Sarah said, and hurled it through their door. The rush matting caught at once. The rest was terrible history.

Abby's trembling hand rattled the oil lamp, and she used the other to still it. Some yards from the open hut door, she set it down, not wishing to alert Hook-Hand to her approach. She glanced about for a weapon, and her eyes alighted on a thick length of timber.

It was too bulky to wield in one hand, so she clasped it in both and raised it above her head, advancing silently.

At the door, she stopped and dared to peer inside.

A wall sconce lit the cluttered space: crates and buckets brimming with theatrical props and discarded equipment. She paid them no heed, her eyes fixed instead on the broad back and sandy hair of the colossus kneeling before her, rummaging in a crate.

Should she warn him, or simply knock him senseless from behind?

The latter seemed wisest. Were he prepared, she stood no chance.

As she eased herself through the doorway, her elbow clipped the edge, knocking it ajar.

The creak gave her away.

Hook-Hand swivelled, wide blue eyes gazing in fear at the lofted club.

"Don't hit me!" he cried, voice cracking.

Abby was already bringing the thick timber down, when something stopped her.

Trevelyan's eyes, she remembered, were green.

Her hands went limp, and the club clattered to the floor.

"Wh-who are you?" the man asked, pushing himself unsteadily to his feet.

Abby's mind was a blur. "You're not Henry Trevelyan."

"Nay, I am not." For a big man, he had a reedy voice and a nervy demeanour. "I'm Harry Gibbons. I assist here on performance days."

It was then that she noticed his hands – both of them. "You… You had a hook-hand. I saw it."

Gibbons reached into the crate and held it up. "A prop from The Young Admiral. I thought it might be amusing to wear it. If 'tis the reason you attacked me, I dearly wish I had not."

When Abby introduced herself – as the new Franny Jenkins, no less – Gibbons managed a smile. The footsteps overhead had grown in intensity, and Tresillion's muffled voice could be heard marshalling his troops.

"We'd best get you back to your company," Gibbons said, ushering her from the storage hut.

As they stepped out, she caught sight of a door to her left, set into the south wall. "Where does that lead?" she asked.

"An old tunnel. It ends at a disused stable block off Drury Lane. Nobody walks it."

Glancing back at the other huts, she allowed herself to be led toward the auditorium.

She had run a fool's errand – but perhaps it had not been in vain.

Chapter Forty

Mr Leyre

"Who's that you're with?" the advancing Fletcher demanded, cane swinging at his side.

Jacob pressed back into his seat, wishing himself anywhere but the Duke's Playhouse.

Lansmere rose smoothly, all practised *hauteur*. "Gresham's man. I assumed you'd know him."

Fletcher was upon them now. He had grown a curious moustache since their last meeting, but Jacob all too easily recognised the crimson cheeks and ferocious stare.

"Be upstanding, damn you!" he snapped. "Show your face."

It was the moment Jacob had dreaded.

Best be done with it, he thought with a sigh, rising in stutters.

Fletcher leaned in, one eyelid twitching.

"Gresham's man?" Lansmere asked Fletcher, tinged with doubt.

Fletcher licked his lips. "Leave us, will you, Benedict?"

It was no request.

"Do I know you, sir?" Fletcher asked. "I sense we have met before."

Jacob stepped from the shadows and bowed so low that his periwig slipped off.

Recognition flashed in Fletcher's eyes. "You're that dandy pratt who turned up uninvited at my house on Clink Street."

The inquisitor retrieved the wig from the floor. "Aye, sir. 'Twas…

"Speak up, man! When was it?"

"The night of the fire, sir."

Fletcher's eyes narrowed. "You came with that girl who accosted me last night. The actress. Accusing me of all manner of dire nonsense. Damned impudence…"

Jacob saw his cheeks flush and his fists clench.

"We… We no longer speak," the inquisitor said, hoping to defuse him.

It seemed to work; Fletcher caught himself. "Gah," he blustered. "Then what is your purpose here? You work for Gresham, you say?"

With Lansmere gone, Jacob felt it best to speak plainly. "Nay, sir. I work for…"

Then he remembered: it was Fletcher's wife's supposed liaisons with Pepys that had sparked the whole disastrous chain of events.

Jacob plucked a name from the ether. "I work for Mr Jacob Leyre."

"And who is this Mr Leyre, pray? What is his trade? And who might you be?"

Too many questions at once, which Jacob parried with fumbled fabrications. He was still amazed that Fletcher had not yet tried to throttle him, as he had last time.

The Duke's manager jabbed his cane into the floor. "I ask again – and I am not accustomed to asking a third time, sir – what is your business here?"

Having told him that Mr Leyre was a bird-catcher, Jacob now found himself at a loss.

His thoughts tumbling like grain in a mill, he simply came out with it. "I did wonder… Did you send Henry Trevelyan to set fire to the Baxter home on Pudding Lane?"

He found himself on his back, ears ringing. Fletcher had caught him across the skull with the silver tip of his cane, so swiftly he had barely seen it coming.

When he tried to rise, he felt a weight on his chest. Fletcher was straddling him, face spitting fury, inches from his own.

That, he thought, dazed, *is the expression I remember.*

"Who sent you?" Fletcher snarled, all sherry-breath and lavender. Dispensing with the cane, he seized Jacob by the throat.

"I came of my own accord," Jacob croaked.

Fletcher shook his head, fingers tightening. "Are you Tresillion's agent, here to besmirch my good name with foul slander?"

"Nnn... snn..." Jacob wheezed, unable to speak.

He fought for breath, but found none. Fletcher's face above him blurred, a cloud of pure ire. He kicked, gripped his assailant's wrists, tried to wrench them free, but Fletcher held the strength of a man possessed.

The light in the room seemed to dim.

A strange weightlessness overtook Jacob, and everything grew dark.

Is this it? he wondered. *Is this how I perish?*

With one final, almighty effort, he prised Fletcher's hands apart and cried out, "Stop!"

It was as if a spell had lifted.

Fletcher shot to his feet, mumbling to himself and scratching distractedly at the sides of his head.

When he looked down and saw Jacob gulping in mouthfuls of air, his eyes flew open in horror. "Oh my Lord, forgive me, sir. I know not what overcame me."

Blabbering apologies, he hauled the inquisitor to his feet and dusted him down.

"Think nought of it," Jacob managed, feeling at his throat. "I-I really must be on my way."

Keen to escape the madness, he turned.

"Nay, sir, I beseech you," Fletcher said, catching at his arm. "Tarry a moment."

Jacob pulled away. *Not for all the jewels in the Tower!*

"The truth is, Mr Standish, this matter of Trevelyan has troubled me also."

It stopped the inquisitor in his tracks.

Fletcher gabbled on. "I am acquainted with Henry Trevelyan, 'tis true, and I assume 'tis where this outrageous tale of fire-raising was kindled. I did indeed send him to Baxter's, though with strict instructions, which it seems he may have ignored. Yet I cling to doubt, for he is a man of his word.

"All London believes the fire started in Thomas Farriner's bakery on Pudding Lane, which I warrant is the truth. Go to Farriner's – I'm told he is still there, rebuilding – and have him confess his folly in writing. Return it to me, sir, and I shall reward you handsomely."

Chapter Forty-One

Clink Street

2 *September 1666*

The meeting sat uneasily with him.

That babbling oaf… What had he called himself?

Aye, that was it – Jacob Standish.

Standish and that impertinent waif accompanying him – the one James had escorted from the house – they had caught him at an importune moment. Mere minutes after his terrible railing at Beatrix.

He stood now, pacing back and forth in the drawing room.

Had he been too blunt with the fellow? Too quick to judge?

Mention of that dreadful Pepys had set his blood to boil. The rumour Standish spoke of had reached his ears, too: that Pepys had dallied with Beatrix. While he trusted her with his life, such aspersions could only harm his standing. And rumours like that never sprang from nowhere. Often, they began with some small, foolish gesture, a morsel of fact upon which to feed.

It had riled him, and he had reacted in good faith.

Reacted, as was his wont, with anger and outrage.

Beatrix sat behind him, tearful and mute.

He, hands clasped behind his back, stared into the leaping flames in the hearth. All around him were framed portraits and playbills, testaments to his triumphs at the Duke's Company. There, Benedict Lansmere, his finest actor, freshly depicted as King Henry astride a stout charger; there, a notice of the debut performance at his Lincoln's Inn Field Theatre: Mr Shakespeare's Macbeth.

It was Lady Macbeth's line that had so scored his heart that night: "My hands are of your colour, but I shame to wear a heart so white."

The line had come back to him a week ago, the night Beatrix had miscarried.

The child they both craved, yet had long considered a fantasy, had been within touching distance.

Then cruelly torn away.

It had broken them both, and they had barely spoken since.

Until tonight, when his frustration and grief had gushed forth.

Gushed forth upon his poor, quailing wife.

He had stormed about the room, sweeping books from their shelves, all sense forsaken. The Macbeth playbill had caught his eye, and that line had come back to him, as if by divine intervention.

"My hands are of your colour, but I shame to wear a heart so white."

His hands were not bloodied, like Lady Macbeth's. Nor like Beatrix's, curled upon the bedsheets that sorrowful night he had lost his heir.

Was it his heart that glowed white, after all?

Then James had appeared in the doorway with news of unexpected guests.

Standish and that girl.

He had not had time to calm himself.

Had he erred in dismissing Standish so curtly?

Worse, still suffused with rage, he had summoned that brute, Trevelyan, who had left moments ago.

Trevelyan's services had come highly recommended. He had dispatched him to Pudding Lane with one instruction: "If the Baxters have Pepys's diaries, bring them to me."

That was all.

Yet the two men had never met before, and Trevelyan's appearance had troubled him. Unnerved him, even, were he man enough to admit it.

That sharpened steel hook. That jawline forged in enmity.

Could he be trusted?

What if he took matters into his own hands?

Edmund looked to his wife, still seated behind him.

Her tears had dried, as she blankly stared.

Chapter Forty-Two

The Gift

As Abby passed Matt Tibbet's workshop, she noticed the door ajar and the padlock lying open in its clasp. She had wondered more than once whether he was guarding his worldly possessions, or perhaps had something more devious to hide.

To her right, in the middle of the tiring-house, a disagreement was threatening to boil over. Marwood, Lucius and Faybourne were surrounding Thomas Tresillion, each demanding to know where their owed monies were.

"I shall not grace that stage till the debt is paid!" Marwood said.

Tresillion let out an exaggerated laugh.

"I side with Peregrine," said Lucius.

"Aye. I, too," said Faybourne.

Others began to gather, some stamping their feet, others shouting encouragement to parties unknown.

The manager's voice rose above the din. "Will you deny the King his entertainment?"

"Traitors!" cried one, while others booed with gusto.

By Abby's reckoning, the drapes would open on The Masque of Sighs in little over three hours.

Spying Tibbet among the crowd, she made a snap decision. Ducking inside his workshop, she eased the door closed behind her.

With no windows, the single room was lit by candles dotted haphazardly about. The air was thick with dust and the oily whiff of paint. Shelves lined the walls, weighed down by piled boxes, jars and cups filled with all manner of everything: nails, cloth, candle stubs, spools of twine, hinges, wig pins, glass beads, scraps of wood too broken to appear useful… Tibbet was a hoarder.

Rope coils, ribbons, chains, a small bell and a soldier's doublet missing one sleeve hung from nails around the walls. A battered workbench was equally cluttered, strewn with tools, half-mended props and a bottle of rum, near empty and cork-less.

All that was too obvious, Abby reasoned. Even with the lock on the door, Tibbet would keep his secrets hidden.

But where?

Comforted by the continuing commotion outside, she swivelled on her heels, eyes darting every which way.

Then she saw it.

The workbench bore a lower shelf, the space beneath it screened by a grubby curtain.

Abby knelt, pushed the curtain aside, and shook her head at what she discovered.

The wooden doll's house looked as though someone had taken a hammer to it. Its floors and walls were riven and splintered, its tiny pieces of furniture crushed flat. On one long stray shard, perhaps from the missing roof, she noticed writing.

She picked it out. Painted there in crude lettering were the words: *For Alice & Jane.*

Tibbet's daughters? Is this a gift he had crafted for them? Then why destroy it?

A sudden howl of outrage from outside made her realise she had lingered too long. She should leave, before the men made their peace.

And she would have done, had a thought not struck her.

With some difficulty, since even in tatters it was heavy, Abby slid the doll's house out from its hiding place and peered into the space behind. It was so gloomy, she grabbed a candle and cast its light inside.

There, against the back wall, lay a bundle of papers tied with string, and a ceramic jar covered with muslin.

Sucking in a breath, she stretched out an arm and retrieved both.

Feverishly, panicking now, she unpicked the string. The rolled papers were letters, torn in half. There was writing scrawled over them, in thick, angry lines.

Still she could read the words beneath.

The letter at the very top of the sheaf began:

Matthew,
You will never see your children again.

It was all Abby needed to know.

Tossing it back into its hiding place, she reached for the jar.

That was when she heard it - a jaunty whistle, and footsteps drawing closer.

The tiring-house, she realised with a start, had fallen all but silent.

The whistling stopped, replaced by the rasp of Matt Tibbet's laboured breathing.

The handle of his workshop door began to turn.

Abby curled into a ball and squeezed her eyes tight shut.

"Tibbet!"

Tresillion's call.

The handle stilled, then turned back.

"On my way, sir."

Temples pounding, Abby whipped off the muslin.

Inside was a thick, white cream, smeared where fingers had scooped through the edge.

She would not dream of tasting it.

Chapter Forty-Three

Monsieur Hubert

Jacob's priority was to find Mr Pepys at Seething Lane, to decipher Franny Jenkins's diary. Since the late actress had seen fit to conceal her innermost thoughts - which, as a resident of The Cock, seemed prudent - there must be secrets locked within. They might even identify her murderer.

Yet a trip to Thomas Farriner's on Pudding Lane would entail but the slightest detour from his route from Lincoln's Inn Field. Indeed, so close was it to Seething Lane that he could hire a hackney coach to Farriner's, then walk to Pepys's.

Jacob sighed. He could not disguise the fact that he had inadvertently secured employment from the very man Abby despised and distrusted the most. She would likely murder him... *if he told her.*

He resolved not to.

Jacob shuddered at his first sight of Pudding Lane. This once-thronged street, lined with shops and tenements, was now a tangle of half-cleared rubble, rough timber huts and smoking braziers.

Masons and labourers had thrown up lodgings from whatever they could scavenge: canvas stretched over scorched beams, soot-blackened bricks stacked into crude shelters. The stench of coal smoke and thawed midden hung in the air.

Hammers clattered and playing children shrieked, yet it all sounded strangely subdued.

The last time Jacob had walked up this street, the fire was just catching. He remembered the screams, the pall of black smoke, the skittering sparks - and his helplessness.

But what could he have done? People had been trying to dig down to a water pipe as he arrived, desperate to fight the flames. The passage of time had proved their efforts in vain.

Anyway, it had been his first mission for Mr Pepys, and he was duty-bound, compelled elsewhere.

Still it pained him.

The baker, Thomas Farriner, was indeed rebuilding his shop, though the tiresome rubble clearance and recent harsh weather had clearly delayed his efforts.

A shallow trench had been dug around the perimeter, filled with rough stones bound by lime mortar. From this rose scaffold poles – tall, upright saplings – like the frame of a giant wicker basket. At the heart of the fledgling bakery, a young woman was on her hands and knees, scrubbing the stone slabs that formed its floor.

Could it be… Did he know her?

As Jacob stepped inside between scaffold poles, she looked up.

Aye, he remembered the face. How could he forget it? The soft cheeks, now smeared with grime, and pert, upturned nose.

"Sarah Baxter?" he asked.

She gasped and threw a hand to her mouth. "You're the man from that night. That dreadful night."

For a moment, he feared she was about to embrace him.

"Aye," he said. "My colleague and I…"

"The young lady?"

"Abigail. We found you here with your daughter… The fire…"

She buried her face in her hands. "It still burns in my mind, sir."

"Jacob. My name is Jacob."

She rubbed her cheeks, steadying herself. "There was nought could be done, Jacob. That foul conflagration… 'Twas sent by the Devil himself, I'll warrant."

It reminded him why he was there. He glanced right, where the remains of the Baxter home – heaps of debris and charred timber stumps – lay untouched.

She noticed, and said quickly, "We're moving to Kent. My husband has kin there."

Jacob turned back to the bakery, brow furrowed. "Then why...?"

She wiped her forehead with a sleeve. "I'm helping Tom, ere we leave Monday week. We've been staying..."

He cut her off. "Tom? Thomas Farriner? The baker, whom London blames for the fire. Yet you..."

She squinted at him. "Why are you here?"

"You told us a man with a hooked hand started it. He threw a torch inside your house."

With a wail, Sarah Baxter threw herself at Jacob's feet, clutching the hem of his coat. "Nay, sir. Don't tell anyone, sir, I beg you. I was merely shielding him, casting blame on another. I had to. When I saw his bakery in flames, and the fire spreading so fast, and then you appeared, and you'd been asking questions that very night..."

He grasped her beneath each shoulder, trying to haul her up, but she resisted.

"I-I panicked," she went on, the words pouring out. "I feared for Tom, didn't I? Folk bay for blood when fire takes hold."

"What's going on here?"

A man had appeared beside them, ruddy-faced, wearing a stout leather apron.

"Tom!" Sarah shot to her feet, flung her arms around his waist, buried her face in his chest and sobbed.

"What have you done to my sister?" Thomas Farriner demanded.

Jacob blinked. "Sister?"

The truth emerged.

The fire had started from a stray ember, left smouldering in an untended oven at Farriner's bakery.

Sarah Baxter had lied to them. Trevelyan had indeed interrogated the Baxters, then left empty-handed, satisfied that Pepys's diaries lay elsewhere.

He never returned. She had lied that night to cover for her brother.

"Will you swear to it?" Jacob asked.

He would appease Edmund Fletcher yet.

Farriner took his sister's hand. "Swear to what?"

"That Trevelyan is devoid of blame."

The baker chuckled. "Have I my liberty?"

Jacob could not decide whether to nod or shake his head, and so simply stared.

"You've not heard?" Farriner added, relishing the inquisitor's confusion. "A man confessed to it. A Frenchman, no less. *Robert Hubert.* Told the court he threw a fire grenade into my bakery, the poor, deluded wretch. They hanged him for it last October." He smiled. "I'm innocent. I'll swear to nought, sir."

Shambles

Tresillion gathered the King's Company for one final rehearsal. By the time it ended, he would wish he had not.

A malaise hung over the Theatre Royal; every sound echoed about the roof beams like a cackle of madness, haunting the production.

The Fates were not aligned.

Cues were missed, marks overstepped, and the prompter was called upon so often he lost his own place. A row ensued, and he quit the theatre in disgust. His replacement was a timid man nobody could hear.

Marwood was in a foul mood, which might have suited the Spirit of Power, had he not refused to play the part. Instead, he stood centre-stage, arms folded, tight-lipped. Tresillion indulged his silent protest, no doubt assuming he would be unable to resist the lure of the audience's adulation once the play began in earnest.

An audience that would include the King himself.

But Abby was not so sure.

Lucius was his usual ebullient self. Perhaps buoyed by Marwood's absence, he seemed to sense all attention on him, and began hamming up his role as the Spirit of Love. He pranced when he should have stridden, gurned when he should have puckered, and overplayed every line.

So unintentionally farcical was he that Faybourne, not to be outshone, began matching him gesture for gesture, until his Spirit of Folly – a tragicomic role, requiring a deft touch – resembled more a fairground mummer.

Even the walk-ons seemed affected. Somebody trod on the trailing hem of Clara Lovick's gown; instead of a grand regal entrance, she fell in a heap then fled the stage.

Meanwhile, Pip's nerves appeared shot. His rash had grown so severe it now seeped through his white shirt, and in his soldier's scene with Lucius's captain, the poor young fellow faltered, gibbered, then was sick down his doublet.

Only Marwood laughed. It was his first utterance.

Abby, her mind elsewhere, could at least fare no worse than the genuine players. She remembered her lines and missed but a single cue.

Lucius, even more pleased with himself than usual, bounded over to congratulate her. He lifted her off her feet and planted a kiss full on her lips, while she glanced about, mortified.

Everyone stared, some more reproachfully than others.

Abby was deeply relieved when the second practice of her flying scene was cancelled.

Tresillion had been adamant it would go ahead, but Pip, sympathetic to her fears having suffered his own, came to her rescue, and convinced the manager that time was too short.

Abby was delighted when Tresillion finally relented.

With time slipping by and the drapes soon to part, she had work to do.

Chapter Forty-Five

Hell

As the company disappeared into the wings, restless and despondent, Abby slipped down into the pit and pressed her back to the apron wall. When she felt sure that every soul had returned to the tiring-house, she opened the understage door and crept inside.

Only then did she notice the word scratched into the timber: HELL.

The lamp Harry Gibbons had used to light their path still glowed by the doorway. She picked it up and closed the door gingerly behind her. Then she stood for a while, ears strained for any sound.

None came.

She was alone.

All she could hear was the beating of her heart and the sputtering of the flame.

Tiptoeing toward the rear of the vast, dingy space, she brushed aside a cobweb.

It reminded her of the state of Orange Bess's clothing when she lay dead and distant-gazed. Bess may have been dusting and cleaning, but the royal box, where Abby had met her, looked already spotless.

The only place in the theatre with cobwebs was here, beneath the stage.

This, Abby had decided, was where Bess was murdered, then dragged out into the pit to cover the perpetrator's tracks.

The old woman had vowed to conduct her own investigation.

It had led to her death.

There were six doors, to six dilapidated, windowless huts. Having already seen inside one, five remained.

What she sought, she could not have said. But she would know it when she saw it.

She began at the far left.

The first hut was so crammed with large sections of scenery that she could scarcely set a foot inside.

The second showed signs of fire damage.

The third, she had already visited.

The fourth perked her interest. It was empty, save for a small desk and chair, the desk spread with old broadsides and playbills. Somebody had clearly used it as a retreat from the mayhem overhead, perhaps skiving from their duties. Yet the floor was thick with ash, and the air reeked of stale tobacco. Something about it felt wrong. Abby checked the desk drawer anyway, and found it empty.

Even as the fifth door juddered open, a rush of herbal scents suffused her nostrils. This hut had been used recently, and likely often. Everyone at the theatre took care of their perfume.

It was heaped with broken furniture - chairs and stools missing legs, an upended chaise longue, a battered old armoire - yet this felt like the place.

Abby stood massaging her chin, staring at the pile, wondering what she was missing. This seemed no refuge for a murderer.

She opened the armoire and peered inside. Empty, with barely room for one to stand.

Yet it was the only thing in the hut that drew her inquisitor's eye.

She was about to close the door when she stopped.

Leaning in, she rapped on the rear panel. Nothing.

She rapped again, harder.

It shifted.

A hidden door.

Stepping through into darkness, her breathing shallow and fitful, Abby wafted her lamp about the tiny space. It was a mess. Only the lingering perfume and the cracked looking glass on one wall reassured her that somebody lately came here.

Clothing lay scattered across the floor, tangled with wide strips of linen and stuffed into two sacks. Among it she found a scented lace handkerchief, a silver spoon bearing the Duke's coat of arms, the scabbard of the prop dagger that had done for Orange Bess, and a screwed-up piece of paper. On it was written:

We must speak
Bess

Her death warrant.

In the far corner, nibbled by rats, she found a mouldering pile of pamphlets. Flipping through them with quavering fingers, she saw the theatrical reviews had been ringed in ink. Wherever Lucius was mentioned by name, it had been underlined.

"Lucius held the crowd in his hand, and quaffed their applause like wine" was ringed three times, as if with a flourish.

She was about to replace the pile when something shimmered dully among the dirt. A small iron key.

She kept it.

Closing the door to the fifth hut, she froze at the sound of faint, muffled footsteps to her left. Somebody was in the tunnel that led to Drury Lane. The same tunnel Gibbons had sworn was disused.

Abby ran.

At the apron door, she skidded to a halt and snuffed out the lamp. Quelling her racing heart, she crouched behind a piece of discarded scenery and waited.

A glow of candlelight stopped outside the hut she had just left. She heard the door open… then softly draw closed.

The figure holding the light had been cloaked in shadows.

But Abby felt sure she knew who it was

Chapter Forty-Six

The Lick

Abby stopped briefly, furtively, at Tibbet's workshop, unnoticed amid the fevered preparations, before hastening to her tiring-room. She almost collided with Thomas Tresillion.

Short as he was, he could still look down on her. His stained teeth were gritted and sweat dribbled in rivulets from his brow.

It's not only the players losing the plot, she thought.

"Where've you been?" he snarled. "You're covered in filth."

Faybourne, in full stage attire, happened to be passing. "She's no actress," he said. "I'd wager good coin she's a spy."

"At this point, Hugh, I couldn't care if she were Cromwell's own spymaster," Tresillion shot back. Then to Abby, he ordered, "Get dressed. And be quick."

Throwing out his arms, he announced to the room, "The King's Company performs before His Majesty in one half hour!"

She had to squeeze past heaving chests and stiff backs to reach her Queen's robe, hanging on its nail. The tiring-room reeked of sweat and apprehension, even though most of those crammed inside had no lines and served merely as stage decoration. They clamoured for space at the looking glasses, eyeing one another with lordly disdain.

Having been so caught up in her inquisitor's duties, Abby was struck suddenly by the weight of what she was about to do. Now she was Abigail Harcourt, principal actor again – albeit relegated to the walk-ons' tiring-room – set to perform at the Theatre Royal for the entertainment of His Majesty King Charles and several hundred baying Londoners.

Her stomach turned over, her head swam, and she glanced about for a friendly face.

She saw only Clara Lovick.

The blonde actress noticed her staring and elbowed others aside to reach her.

"Hate to see your flying contraption fail," she hissed in Abby's ear, then licked it, leering.

Chapter Forty-Seven

The Masque of Sighs

Stepping onto the stage for her first scene felt like wading through tar. Something compelled Abby forward, even as her leaden feet resisted. The air seemed to pulse.

The stage had been set: the floorboards strewn with petals and leaves, around a stone bench draped in ivy. The glade.

Queen Seraphina enters, and first encounters the Spirit of Love. On the eve of her royal betrothal, she is uncertain, yearning for clarity. Love states his case, lays claim to her allegiance.

She knew all this.

Then why did the task ahead feel insurmountable?

I'm a charlatan, that's why!

The revelation hit her like a charging boar.

She was no actress!

Abby heard herself laugh, then came a wave of noise in her left ear. Cheers, whistles, hoots, and a braying, stately voice calling out, "What's under your petticoats?"

Mr Pepys had inveigled her into his simple-minded scheme, and she had convinced herself she could cope. Only the Lord knew how she had managed to rise from servant to inquisitor. By the skin of her teeth, that was how.

And now he expected her to transform from inquisitor into actress, as the caterpillar becomes a butterfly.

It can't be done.

Why on earth had she thought otherwise? Simply knowing the lines did not an actor make.

Abby's head dropped to her chest.

When she raised it, a thousand eyes stared back at her.

Who are all these people?

Through her fogged mind, she noticed urgent movement among the crowd: a hand waving.

She followed the hand up the arm to the shoulder, and came upon a face.

It was a face she recognised. Red hair, blue-green eyes, cheeky grin.

Will. Her brother.

Whoomph.

That boar again.

She was standing on the apron of the King's Playhouse in London, staring out at a packed house. Every seat, she had been told, was sold. The debut performance of the much-fêted Mr Sawyer's Masque of Sighs.

The hottest ticket in Westminster.

Her eyes were drawn upwards. And there he was: King Charles, a broad grin on his lascivious lips, and a pouting lady draped over each shoulder.

Abby's gaze returned to the audience. Where were Jacob and Mr Pepys?

Everybody was so strangely silent.

All waiting for her.

Waiting for Abigail Harcourt to utter her opening line.

If only she could remember it.

Chapter Forty-Eight

Hush

An old man seemed to whisper from somewhere in the wings, and she could barely make out his words. Only "dreams"… and "taunt".

That useless prompter, she realised.

Yet he had stirred a memory.

For the first time, she heard it: the melancholic strains of a lute, playing beneath her feet.

A buck-toothed fop, lolling over the stage as if he owned it, stood upright and coughed loudly.

"It appears the Queen has lost her tongue! If His Majesty has his way," Edward Eversleigh paused, "she may well lose her head!"

Uproar. Fruit flew, a bench in the pit toppled, and the King rose to his feet, bowing over his rolling hand.

"You wear strange faces, yet I know your voices from my dreams. Why do you taunt me so?"

The line came in a low rumble, spoken through gritted teeth.

Abby followed the voice and saw Lucius waiting in a wing, urging her on with frantic gestures.

"You wear strange faces…" she heard herself cry out.

Heads turned.

"Not as strange as Everseligh's!" some wag quipped, to gales of laughter.

She ignored it. "You wear strange faces, yet I know your voices from my dreams. Why do you taunt me so?"

The barracking subsided.

"The wind holds still, the birds forget their song. As if the very world doth hush for me."

And in that moment, it had.

Abby exhaled, for what felt like an eternity.

As she did so, a figure in the front of the pit caught her attention. All eyes were on her - his bored right through her, reaching for her very soul. His long grey periwig and downturned hat obscured much of his face, yet she knew those haunting eyes. That ridiculous moustache.

Edmund Fletcher.

He tipped his hat and smiled.

"What summons sighs 'neath so bright a sky? Who warrants pity when joy is yet to hand?"

Lucius's voice again.

He was beside her now, down on one knee, head bowed in reverence.

She took his hand, lifting him to his feet. "Love's Spirit? I had hoped for peace, not riddles."

And in that instant, Fletcher, Pepys, Jacob, Will, Franny Jenkins, Matt Tibbet, Orange Bess… All were forgotten.

Chapter Forty-Nine

Flight

Abby had made it.

London loved her.

Why, one well-heeled gent had even hauled himself onto the stage mid-scene to offer her a rose.

When she accepted it, the cacophony of applause and stamping feet shook dust from the rafters. How the King's eyes had glistened.

And so, to the final act. The flying scene she dreaded now more than ever.

Tibbet's hands worked at her back in the low light, securing the knots that would keep her from plummeting to the stage. His breath, heavy and pungent, warmed her neck.

"I found the poison," she said, almost carelessly.

"What say you?"

Suddenly his head was beside hers, his stubble rough against her cheek.

"I know you didn't murder her," she added quickly. "I found a key. It fit your lock."

"What's yer game? *Spy?*" He spat the word.

At last, Abby could unburden herself. The truth poured out, like coin from a split purse.

When she finished, Tibbet could only shake his head in admiration. "For an inquisitor, yer make a devilish fine actress. You oughta…"

"I need your help," she cut in. "We don't have long."

A collective gasp rose as Queen Seraphina's feet lifted from the draped platform and she appeared to float, wobbling slightly.

This was what they had paid to see. Tresillion's grand promise.

"A flight never before dared upon the English stage."

"Higher!" someone shouted, to hollered approval.

From one wing came a plaintive cry. "I can't hold it! Somebody help!"

Abby shrieked as she shot upwards at frightening speed - higher than before, twice as high - then jerked to a halt, so far above the stage that the three Spirits below looked no bigger than mice.

Bewildered, she caught sight of a man in the fly gallery to her right, his face white with fear.

"Someone's tampered with the counterweight," he said.

She had no time to respond. With a dull *twang*, one of the strands in the rope linking her harness to the winching line gave way. She dropped a little, then stopped.

She had anticipated this moment. It made it no less terrifying.

The audience had no idea what to make of it. Some marvelled at such a death-defying spectacle, others nudged their neighbour, wide-eyed.

"Abby!"

Jacob's familiar voice cut above the crowd's confusion.

At last, she thought, as another sabotaged strand snapped, and she fell a little further.

Her heart pumped like an overwound clock, and she wailed his name. "Jacob!"

He had left the wheezing Pepys behind even before they reached Bridges Street. Now, as he hurtled into the pit, his worst fears were realised.

"We know the murderer!" he bellowed, scattering folk from their seats as he forced his way toward the stage.

But some were not so easily moved. A pair of burly gentlemen blocked his path, and when he tried to push between them, they wrestled him to the floor.

Helpless, he gazed up at Abby, dangling so very far above the stage, as her rope finally gave way.

And down she came.

"Abby!" he screamed.

Chapter Fifty

Nadir

Matt Tibbet's secondary rope, so hastily secured minutes earlier, was a little longer than Abby would have wished. When the sabotaged line gave way, she knew she would drop further than planned.

In the half-light, he had not noticed the cuts. When she pointed them out... She would not forget his devastated expression, nor his desperate apologies.

She had brushed them aside. "Work fast," she urged.

The sliced rope, she had expected. The added counterweight, she had not - despite Tibbet's earlier tale of an intruder in the rafters.

Double the sabotage. Truly, that was the work of a deranged mind, somebody who dearly wanted her dead.

Yet she had foiled their plan, as she had prayed she would.

But would it flush them into the open?

Masks discarded, Marwood, Lucius and Faybourne stared up at Abby in their robes of different colours. Lucius appeared frantic; Marwood, almost bored.

"Bring her down!" Lucius cried to the man at the winch.

"I can't. The pulley's jammed," came the reply.

Abby's fretful sigh had barely left her lips when a figure came hurtling from the wing.

Dressed in soldier's garb, he bowled into Lucius, sending him sprawling.

Both fell to the floor, where Pip Tredwell began beating at Lucius's chest, howling, "Why can't you love me?"

A choke of discomfort rippled through the house.

Oblivious, Pip turned his face upward, glaring at Abby swinging high above, and shook both fists. "And you! Spy! Why did you not die?"

He wrenched open his doublet, sending brass buttons skittering across the stage. "I sacrificed all for my father. I adopted this deceit willingly, that I might join this exalted company of actors."

Lurching to his feet, he tugged at the collar of his linen shirt, as if to rend it.

"All I asked was a little love. From you," he motioned to the audience. "And from you, Mr Lucius, whom I admire more than life itself."

Wordlessly, Lucius opened and closed his mouth.

Out in the house, chairs scraped. One by one, the audience rose.

On the stage, everyone stood rapt, dumbfounded.

Pip tugged again at the shirt, tears of frustration welling in his eyes. "Yet you show affection to anyone but me."

Lucius lifted his head. "I…"

"After half a decade, Mr Lucius, you still forget my name! I am Pip, damn you - not Puck."

His raised voice carried not anger, but pain.

"Look at me!"

Then softer: "Look at me."

And they did. Every one of them.

For the first time in his theatrical life, Pip Tredwell was master of the stage.

The rope juddered, and with silent thanks to a higher power, Abby felt herself being lowered.

Jacob, she saw, had stopped struggling, also transfixed. Mr Pepys was just arriving, clearly taken aback by the hush that had gripped the auditorium.

But Pip was not finished.

He strode to the front of the apron and stared out into the crowd. When his gaze met someone's, they looked away. None among them could bear it.

Eversleigh opened his mouth to speak, and Pip silenced him with a look.

"What do you see when you gaze on me? A walk-on!" He laughed bitterly. "A young man at the very nadir of his powers!"

A few dared the briefest of nods. Others hung their heads.

"Well, you're all wrong!"

It landed like a sword blow.

"I am no man, you see. I'm no Phillip."

Taking a handful of shirt in each fist, he ripped the garment in two, exposing a wide band of cloth wrapped tight around his chest.

"I am Phillipa Tredwell!"

One lady fainted.

Abby landed with a *thud*, lost her balance, and toppled.

Phillipa turned, snarled, and flung herself at the sprawled inquisitor. "But for you and your questions, Abigail Harcourt!"

As the actors stood frozen in shock, Jacob leapt onto the stage and threw himself at Phillipa, Will Harcourt close behind.

Feeling Will's arms lock around his waist, trying to pull him back, he struggled. The two men rolled sideways, grappling and cursing.

Abby, meanwhile, fought off Phillipa's flailing arms.

Then disaster struck.

Jacob's elbow caught one of the tall candelabra set for the flying scene. Down it crashed, sending a dozen candles scattering across the stage.

One came to rest at the foot of a drape, and in seconds, it was alight.

No one moved. They could only stare as flame licked up the red velvet, climbing fast.

Then, from nowhere, a figure hurtled in and seized the drape. Clutching it to his chest, he threw himself to the stage, wrenching it from its fittings. It fell in a heap, and he rose, stamping out the flames with spurred boots.

With a swish, Edmund Fletcher removed his hat and bowed.

The audience erupted.

Delirium.

Flowers were thrown. Coins. Hats. Gloves. A lady's stockings.

Never had the King's Playhouse known such scenes.

The stage itself throbbed, as if with the heartbeat of London.

Into this maelstrom, hesitantly, from a wing, came Thomas Tresillion.

He stopped, dumbstruck and open-mouthed.

"I expected a disaster and could not bear to watch," he told the nearest actor. "What did I miss?"

Chapter Fifty-One

Curtain

Samuel Pepys was in the gayest of moods. The King had been appraised of Abby's exploits at the playhouse, and had afterwards congratulated him on his choice of inquisitor.

The less said about Jacob, the better. Pepys had not addressed a single word to him since they took their table at The Cock.

The irony that Fletcher - whom Abby had feared would burn down the theatre - should be the one to extinguish the fire was lost on neither of them. It, too, remained unspoken.

"How did you know it was Pip?" Pepys asked Abby, as Oxford Kate replenished their mugs with warm, spiced sack. Tresillion having insisted on paying, he made sure his was properly filled.

Abby took a deep slug. Her knees had only recently stopped quaking from her ordeal. "She came into the tiring-room while I was dressing, before the second day's rehearsal. Yet she didn't dress, only took a pinch of snuff and asked after my discourse with Orange Bess. Bess was a wily old bird who saw everything. The next day, she was dead.

"And it struck me - I never saw Pip dress in the tiring-room."

"Aye," Jacob added, glancing nervously at Pepys. "Our first day in the King's playhouse, Mr Pepys and I saw Pip arrive in stage attire. He was late, and cold. Franny Jenkins brushed dust from his... from her doublet."

Abby grinned at him. "Precisely. Where did she dress, if not in the tiring-room? The cobwebs on Bess led me to the understage, where I found Pip's den. She worshipped Lucius, hoarded notices of his triumphs. In this very tavern, one of the old walk-ons had jested, 'Reckon Pip's in love with Lucius.' If only I had known how true those words were.

"The more Lucius rebuffed her, the more unhinged she grew. That he flirted with me only enraged her, and she stepped between us more than once - for which, at the time, I was grateful. That rash on her arm was merely an outward sign. Inwardly, the poor woman was in turmoil."

Pepys rose, scowling. "Poor woman? That *poor woman* murdered Franny and Bess. She..."

Before he could continue, Thomas Tresillion flopped into one of the spare chairs at the table. His eyes were crossed, and he seemed very drunk.

"How fare we, fine folk?" he asked, throwing an arm around Pepys.

Pepys patted him heartily on the back. "Most excellently, kind sir. And we are most grateful for the flowing sack you have provided."

Tresillion belched.

"You're uncommonly generous with your coin, Mr Tresillion," Abby said.

"We do what we can," he slurred.

She leaned in, her turquoise eyes glinting. "Lavish costumes, the finest scenery, wine for all…"

Tresillion nodded, grinning blissfully.

"…Yet your players go unpaid."

He drew closer, attempting a wink that was more of a blink, and tapped his ruddy nose. "There may be some minor… *mismanagement*, I confess."

It was all Abby could do not to glance at Pepys, so assured had he been of financial motives for the Drury Lane murders. She heard him clear his throat.

Tresillion reached for Abby's hand, but she did not oblige him. "My good friend, Edmund Fletcher, has offered to assist with my… accounting procedures, my dear," he said. "Pray, do not trouble your pretty little head."

With that, he lurched to his feet, pointed himself vaguely at his table, and fell over.

Abby allowed herself a quiet chuckle.

A feast arrived at the company's tables: roasted pork, mutton pies, pickled eggs, smoked herring and trenchers of bread.

Pepys produced Franny Jenkins's diary, purloined by Jacob. The inquisitor begged him to keep it from Oxford Kate's eagle eye, fearing her wrath.

Pepys ignored him. "Here," he said, jabbing at a page. "It says, 'Pip tells me Lansmere tried to kiss him last night. Most unwise. Poor Benedict could lose his head. Pip seems eager to be rid of him, to make room for his precious Dorian. What a fool. A walk-on. I must use this knowledge wisely.'"

He closed the diary and returned it to his satchel. "And use it, she did. If only Lansmere had known."

"He sent Pip gifts," Jacob ventured.

"A silver spoon and a goblet," Abby said. "Both bearing the Duke of York's label."

Pepys inspected a pickled egg. "And she wished you dead."

Abby grimaced at the memory. "I'd asked too many questions. She knew I was a spy. After Lucius kissed me, she urged Tresillion to forego another rehearsal of my flying scene. She'd sabotaged the counterweight and rope the previous night, and preferred that I perish before a packed house. I fear she may be quite mad."

"Is that why she lived as a man?" Jacob asked.

Abby's mouth fell open. "She had no choice, Jacob. 'Twas her father's dying wish that she join the King's Company, and she did so… perhaps mere days before the King allowed women on the stage. Having entered the company as Phillip, she was stuck with him."

"She'll hang," said Pepys.

Abby gazed upwards. "A tragic end to our investigation."

Jacob, pleased to hear his contribution acknowledged, set down the slice of pie he was holding. "Mr Pepys?"

"What is it, Jacob Standish? About to ask what I have planned for you next? If so, it would be most presumptuous of you. Your conduct at the King's Playhouse today was…"

An ink-stained hand reached into the table, retrieving Jacob's discarded pie.

"May I be of service, sir?" Will Harcourt asked, sliding into a seat beside Pepys.

Jacob all but recoiled.

"I heard you were celebrating," Will said through a mouthful of mutton. "Hope you don't mind me joining you?"

Pepys shifted in his chair. "I, ah, feared this moment would come. I am aware you wish to become my inquisitor, William?"

He nodded eagerly, almost childlike.

Pepys could barely disguise his disdain. "While the decision is mine - and mine alone - since you carry with you my good name, I would wish to hear Abigail's thoughts on the matter. For it is she who must rely upon your aptitude in the role."

Jacob shrank back. Will beamed as he heartily chewed.

So this is it, thought Jacob.

How dearly he cherished being Mr Samuel Pepys's inquisitor, and felt honoured to have been chosen. How boundlessly his respect and regard for Abby had grown during their all-too-brief time together.

He would miss the role - and her - terribly.

It had made a man of him, it had…

"I choose Jacob," he heard.

"And I would choose Jacob over any man in the realm," Abby went on. "He is decent, honest, brave, and a hundred times the inquisitor my brother could ever wish to be."

"But sis…" How Will's face fell.

"Forgive me, Will, but I can't trust you. I wish you well - but I wish you gone."

"Sis!" He was on his feet, hands wringing.

Pepys rose, too. "You have heard her choice, William Harcourt. Now begone, would you."

He spat as he left. "You'll be sorry. All of you."

Jacob waved.

There was no triumph in Abby's face, only sadness.

Tresillion's generosity heartily indulged, the three tucked into Oxford Kate's marchpane and posset, each of them slightly the worse for wear.

Pepys, seeing how his inquisitors were itching for their next investigation, beckoned Abby and Jacob closer.

"I…" He cleared his throat. "I… misplaced some gold. At a time of great peril, when the Dutch fleet did sail brazenly up the Thames."

Their eyes lit up.

"Misplaced?" Abby asked.

"'Twas buried. By my father and sister. In the garden at Brampton."

Abby and Jacob exchanged a glance. Were they to return to the Huntingdonshire countryside? Reacquaint themselves with a few old faces?

"And when I came to dig it up…" Pepys hesitated. "Well, 'twas gone."

"Stolen?" Jacob asked.

"A tale stalking the paths of the village suggests as much. And that…" He stopped, as if unsure.

Abby reached for Jacob's hand. "And that what, sir?"

"And that my bountiful pilfered hoard is now guarded…" Pepys wiped something from his eye. "By a ghost."

"A ghost?" the inquisitors exclaimed in unison.

"Nonsense, no doubt. Ghosts are no more real than the witches you lately investigated. And I trust you shall uncover the flesh and blood behind this most heinous of crimes.

"Whoever it may be."

If you enjoyed this book, please consider leaving a rating or review – they are greatly appreciated and genuinely help.

Next up: deadly old scores are settled when Abby and Jacob return to Brampton, in The Samuel Pepys Mysteries Book 7: The Brampton Ghost Murders.
Amazon link: mybook.to/pepys-series

- "This series just gets better with every book" – *Rambling Mads*

- "A brilliant mix of history and fiction - I loved every minute" – *What You Tolkein About*

- "The Samuel Pepys Mystery series never disap-

points. Every book is well-researched and su-
perbly written" – *Cozy Crime Reads*

Read All Nine!

mybook.to/pepys-series

Ellis Blackwood

Ellis Blackwood fell in love with the writings of Samuel Pepys and the 17th-century England he so colourfully portrays via the great man's published diaries. The Samuel Pepys Mysteries are the result of that literary love affair.

Ellis lives on the coast of Cornwall with his wife, two daughters and dog, Spike. A former journalist, he wrote features for many of the UK's most popular national newspapers and magazines. During the COVID lockdown, he gained an MA in Comedy Writing.

Visit my website ellisblackwood.com for all release updates, and to subscribe to my monthly newsletter – including the FREE Pepys Mysteries introductory novella, Mr Pepys's Stolen Diaries.

Find me on Facebook @ellisblackwoodauthor
And on Instagram @ellisblackwood_author
Scan the QR code for all my links.

Acknowledgements

I could not have published The Samuel Pepys Mysteries without the sterling work of Tim Brown, whose covers are a joy to behold, and whose editorial guidance has been a godsend. Equally, my wife, Sinead, has worked tirelessly and generously in the background to allow me the time and space to research, write, and drink far too much tea.

If you'd like to learn more about Samuel Pepys and 17th century England, I recommend starting here:

- *The Illustrated Pepys* edited by Robert Latham, Penguin Books (1979)

- *London and the 17th Century* by Margarette Lincoln, Yale University Press (2021)

- *Samuel Pepys: The Unequalled Self* by Claire

Tomalin, Penguin Books (2003)

- *The Time Traveller's Guide to Restoration Britain* by Ian Mortimer, The Bodley Head (2017)

In my monthly newsletters, I deep-dive into the fascinating historical background to each novel, from the Princes in the Tower to the ingredients of posset. Visit ellisblackwood.comto sign up.